Th

Shelley raised her [illegible] lowering his hand from the switch on the wall. In the flickering light he appeared larger, stronger, more masculine than ever. The firelight kissed the planes of his face and cast the hollows into deep shadow. The stark contrast made his expression impossible to read, but the predatory gait with which he walked towards her announced his intent.

She unfolded her legs and put her stockinged feet on the floor, as though preparing to run. "I've got one more exam to grade," she said tremulously.

"It can wait. I can't. I've already waited ten years."

ERIN ST. CLAIRE

has worked part-time in commercial television, at one time hosting her own daily show. Well known for her fluid, sensuous style of writing, she has written five novels within eighteen months after her first serious attempt at writing fiction. She is married to a former newscaster and talk show host, and has two small children.

Dear Reader,

SILHOUETTE DESIRE is an exciting new line of contemporary romances from Silhouette Books. During the past year, many Silhouette readers have written in telling us what other types of stories they'd like to read from Silhouette, and we've kept these comments and suggestions in mind in developing SILHOUETTE DESIRE.

DESIREs feature all of the elements you like to see in a romance, plus a more sensual, provocative story. So if you want to experience all the excitement, passion and joy of falling in love, then SILHOUETTE DESIRE is for you.

I hope you enjoy this book and all the wonderful stories to come from SILHOUETTE DESIRE. I'd appreciate any thoughts you'd like to share with us on new SILHOUETTE DESIRE, and I invite you to write to us at the address below:

Jane Nicholls
Silhouette Books
PO Box 177
Dunton Green
Sevenoaks
Kent
TN13 2YE

ERIN ST. CLAIRE

A Kiss Remembered

Silhouette Desire
Published by Silhouette Books

First printing 1984

British Library C.I.P.

St Clare, Erin
A kiss remembered.—(Silhouette desire)
I. Title
813'.54[F]   PS3569.T/

ISBN 0 340 34963 8

The characters and situations in this book are entirely imaginary and bear no relation to any real person or actual happening

Printed and bound in Great Britain for Hodder and Stoughton Paperbacks, a division of Hodder and Stoughton Ltd., Mill Road, Dunton Green, Sevenoaks, Kent (Editorial Office: 47 Bedford Square, London, WC1 3DP) by Richard Clay (The Chaucer Press) Ltd., Bungay, Suffolk

A Kiss Remembered

1

She had purposely chosen a seat near the back of the classroom in order to study him without being obvious. It was remarkable how unchanged he was. Physically, the ten years since they'd seen one another had enhanced his masculine appeal. During his twenties he had held the promise of being a magnetic, virile man; in his thirties that promise had been realized.

Shelley's pen scratched across her tablet as she took notes on his lecture. This was only the second week of the fall semester, but he was already well into the topics he wanted to cover before the final exams just before Christmas. He held the class's rapt attention.

The political-science courses were conducted in

one of the oldest buildings on campus. Its ivy-covered walls suggested a prestigious East Coast university rather than a college located in a north-eastern Oklahoma township. The age of the building, its pleasantly creaking hardwood floors, and high-ceilinged, hushed hallways lent it a sedate atmosphere that appealed to the prelaw students.

The instructor, Grant Chapman, was propped against the desk at the front of the classroom. The desk was solid oak. It had survived over thirty years of professors leaning against it and bore its years well.

As did the man, Shelley thought. Mr. Chapman was as muscularly solid as he had been ten years before. Many a young heart had fluttered when he played on the faculty basketball team against the varsity. Wearing basketball trunks and a tank top, Grant Chapman had rendered the girls of Poshman Valley High School breathless. Shelley Browning included. Ten years had only honed those sleek muscles to a mature strength.

Silver now threaded the dark hair that was just as carelessly styled as it had been then. There had been a stringent rule against long hair at Poshman Valley High School, and the handsome young civics teacher had been one of its most frequent violators.

Shelley could vividly remember the day she'd first heard of Grant Chapman.

"Shelley, Shelley, wait until you see the dreamy new government teacher!" It was enrollment day after summer vacation. Her friend's face was flushed with excitement as she ran up to greet Shelley with the news. "We have him second period and he's absolutely beautiful. And he knows that when you talk about Chicago you're not talking about a city in Illinois. He's young! Government's going to be a gas," the girl had squealed, running off to inform someone else of their good fortune. "Oh, and his name is Mr. Chapman," she had called over her shoulder.

Shelley now listened to the deep resonance of his voice as he answered a question from a student. But his thorough answer didn't register any more than had the question asked him. Shelley was concentrating only on his voice. Leaning over her desk and unobtrusively closing her eyes, she remembered the first time she had heard those low, well-modulated tones.

"Browning, Shelley? Are you here?"

Her heart had plummeted to her feet. No one wanted to be called on the very first day back to school. Twenty pairs of curious eyes were riveted on her. She raised a trembling hand. "Yes, sir."

"Miss Browning, you've already lost your gym shorts. You may pick them up in the girls' locker-room office. Miss Virgil sent a note."

The class broke up and there were several catcalls and whistles. She stammered a thank-you to the new teacher, her cheeks flaming scarlet. He'd think she was a ninny. Funny, his opinion had meant more to her then than had that of her peers.

As she filed out of class that day he had stopped her at the door. "I'm sorry if I embarrassed you," he said apologetically. Her girl friends were standing by, wide-eyed and envious.

"That's all right," Shelley had said timidly.

"No, it's not. You get five grace points on the first exam."

She had never gotten those five extra points because she made a one hundred on the first exam and on most of them after that. Government was her favorite subject that semester.

"Are you talking about before Vietnam or after?" Mr. Chapman was currently asking the student who had inquired about the influence of public opinion on presidential decisions.

Shelley shifted back to the present. He'd never remember "Browning, Shelley" and her lost gym shorts. She doubted if he'd remember at all those four brief months he'd taught at Poshman Valley High School. Surely not after all he'd been through. One didn't climb up through the ranks of Congress to become a valuable senatorial aide by being sentimental. One didn't survive the public scandal Grant Chapman had survived by dwelling on incidents that had happened years earlier in a small farming community that played such an insignificant role in his colorful life.

Maybe that was why he seemed so unchanged to her. She had seen him on television often when reporters were still hounding him for a comment on the scandal that had rocked Washington society. She had studied the pictures of him accompanying the newspapers' headline accounts. Unflattering as newspaper pictures usually were, she could see no deterioration in the face that had emblazoned itself on her mind and refused, even after ten years, to be dismissed.

Shelley was sure he wouldn't know her. At sixteen she had been coltishly slender. No less svelte now, she was softer, rounder, fuller in a very feminine way. The years had melted away the childish plumpness in her face to leave behind an interesting bone structure. High cheekbones accentuated her smoke-blue eyes.

Gone were the long bangs that had characterized her schoolgirl hairstyle. Now her hair was swept back to show her finely arched brows and heart-shaped hairline. A true brunette, she was blessed with richly textured hair that fell over her shoulders like dark wine with sunlight shimmering through it.

Gone was the round-cheeked girl in cheerleader's uniform. Gone also was the innocence, the idealism. The woman was all too aware of the world and its selfishness and injustice. Grant Chapman knew something of that, too. They weren't the same people they had been ten years before, and she asked herself for the thousandth time why she had signed up for his class.

"Consider President Johnson's position at that time," he was saying.

Shelley glanced down at her watch. Only fifteen minutes of the class remained and she had taken exactly two lines of notes. If she weren't careful, she wouldn't excel in this class as she had in the government class that first semester of her junior year.

She recalled a cold windy day after that season's first norther.

"Would you consider helping me grade papers a few afternoons a week?" he had asked.

She was wearing her current boyfriend's letter jacket and her hands were tightly balled into fists inside the deep pockets. Mr. Chapman had stopped her in the courtyard between the gym and the classroom building. His collar-length hair, a shade too long to meet the code, was whipping wildly around his head. Wearing only his sportcoat, he was hunched against the north wind.

"Of course if you'd rather not, just tell—"

"No, no," she rushed to say and licked her lips, hoping they weren't chapped and dry-looking. "Yes, I'd like to. If you think I can."

"You're my champion student. That was a super report you did on the judicial system."

"Thank you." She was flustered and wondered why her heart was pounding so. He was just a teacher. Well, not *just* a teacher.

"If you can grade the objective parts of the tests, I'll read the essays. It'll save me hours of time in the evenings."

She had wondered then what he did in the evenings. Did he see a woman? That had been the topic of speculation at many a slumber party. She'd never seen him in town with anyone.

One night when her family had gone to the Wagonwheel steak house to eat dinner he was there. Alone. When he'd spoken to her, she'd nearly died. She stumbled through introductions to her parents and he'd stood up to shake hands with her father. After they were seated her little brother had spilled his milk and she could have gladly strangled him. When she hazarded a glance toward Mr. Chapman's table, he had left.

"Okay. What days?"

He squinted his eyes against the sunlight, which was bright in spite of the cold. She could never quite decide if his eyes were gray or green or somewhere in between, but she liked the way his dark lashes curled up when his eyes were narrowed that way. "You tell me." He laughed.

"Well, I have cheerleading practice on Thursday because of the pep rallies on Fridays." Stupid! He knows when the pep rallies are. "I take piano on Tuesday." What does he care, Shelley? "I guess Monday and Wednesday would be best."

"That'll be fine," he said. "Whew, it's cold. Let's get inside."

She had nearly tripped over her own stumbling feet when he unexpectedly took her elbow and escorted her to the door of the building. By the time the metal door clanged shut behind them, she thought she might very well faint because he'd touched her. She never told any of her girl friends about that. At the time, it was too precious a secret to tell.

The afternoons spent quietly in his classroom became the pivot around which the rest of her life revolved. She agonized on the days she didn't go, and she agonized on the days she did until the last bell of the day rang. She tried not to rush through the emptying halls to his classroom, but was often breathless when she arrived. Sometimes he wasn't there, but had left her a stack of papers with instructions. She went about grading her classmates' work with a diligence she'd never applied to anything else in her life. Often when he joined her, he'd bring her a soda.

One day as she sat checking the papers with the red pencil he'd given her, he stood up from his desk, where he was reading through an indecipherable composition. He peeled the V-necked sweater he wore over his head. "I think they've got the heat too high in here. This school isn't doing its part to conserve energy."

At the time, she couldn't even admire his patriotic conscientiousness, for she was dazzled by him. He linked his fingers, turned his hands outward and stretched his arms high over his head, arching his back. She was spellbound by the play of muscles under his soft cotton shirt. He released his breath in a healthy sigh as he lowered his arms and rolled his shoulders in an effort to relax them.

Shelley dropped the red pencil, her fingers suddenly useless. Had her skin not been holding her together, she thought she would have melted over the desk. She became aware of a stifling heat that had nothing to do with the thermostat on the wall.

She left his classroom that day bewildered. Much as she wanted to be near him, she suddenly felt compelled to escape. But there was no escaping this assault on her emotions because the tumult was within herself. It was totally new and different and nothing in her dating experiences had prepared her for it. She couldn't identify it then. Only later, when she was older, was she able to define what she had felt that afternoon: desire.

During those days of late fall, he never treated

her with anything but open friendlinesss. When her boyfriend picked her up after football practice to drive her home in his reconditioned Cougar, Mr. Chapman called, "Have fun," to them as they left.

"Before next session you might want to read the first three chapters of the textbook. It's boring as hell, but it will give you good background information."

Shelley was yanked out of her revery by his words. He had one hip hitched over the edge of the desk, a posture that blatantly declared his sex. Shelley doubted that any woman in the room was immune to his overwhelming sexuality. A woman would have to be blind or senile not to be affected, and glancing around, Shelley saw none that fit that description.

Rather, she saw that the female members of the class were all in their late teens or early twenties. High firm breasts jutted braless under T-shirts, and well-shaped, athletic thighs were encased in tight designer jeans. There were skeins of long carelessly styled hair in varying shades of brown, auburn and gold. She felt old and dowdy by comparison.

As you are, Shelley, she reminded herself. She was wearing a sweater, cranberry in color, and she wore a bra beneath it. The sweater matched her textured hose and complemented the mid-calf-length gray wool skirt. At least she knew how to dress fashionably and wasn't consigned to the polyester set—yet.

At twenty-six she was second oldest in the class. A serious gray-haired gentleman was seated in the front row. He had taken copious notes while the young man in the cowboy hat sitting next to Shelley had peacefully napped during the entire hour.

"Good-bye," Mr. Chapman said when the bell rang. "Oh yes, would Mrs. Robins please stop by the desk?"

History was repeating itself.

Shelley all but dropped the armload of books she was gathering up when he made his request. Less interested than the classmates at Poshman Valley had been, the forty or so other students filed out of the classroom, most of them intent on lighting up their first cigarette in over an hour.

Head down, she concentrated on weaving her way through the maze of desks, less ordered than the neat rows in his classroom ten years ago. Out of the corner of her eye, she saw the last student leave the room. Negligently he let the door close solidly behind him. She stifled the insane impulse to ask him to please leave it open.

When she was a few feet away from his desk, when she had run out of excuses not to look at him, she lifted the screen of dark lashes from her eyes and met Grant Chapman's gaze fully for the first time in ten years.

"Hello, Shelley."

She gasped. Or at least she felt the soft gasp rise to her throat and only hoped later that she had caught it in time. "Hello, Mr. Chapman."

A chuckle formed in his throat, but he, too, stopped it before it made a sound. His wide, sensually molded lips smiled easily, but his eyes were busy taking an inventory of her face. They took note of her hair, the unknowingly vulnerable eyes, the slender elegance of her nose, her lips. He studied her lips for a long time, and when her tongue came out nervously to moisten them, she cursed it for doing so.

It was dangerously still and quiet in the room. He had come away from the desk to stand directly in front of her. He had always seemed so overwhelmingly tall. Not frighteningly so, but protectively so.

"I . . . I didn't think you'd know me."

"I knew you the first day you came to class." Standing close like this, his voice sounded huskier. When he projected it during one of his lectures, it lost the intimate pitch that was now wreaking havoc on her equilibrium. "I was starting to wonder if you were going to go through the entire semester without even saying hello."

Ten years of maturity were swept away by his gentle teasing and she felt as young and callow as the first day she met him.

"I didn't want to embarrass you by speaking and having you struggle to remember me. That would have put you in an awkward position."

"I appreciate your concern, but it was unnecessary. I remember you well." He continued to peruse her face analytically and she wondered if he thought the years had embellished or detracted from her features. She herself didn't feel that she had become less attractive or more so; she only knew she was different from the girl who had so painstakingly graded his papers.

Had he known about her infatuation for him? Had he discussed it with a lady friend? "You should see her, sitting there so prim and proper, her hands perspiring. Every time I move, she jumps like a scared rabbit." She imagined him shaking his head ruefully and laughing.

"Shelley?"

He routed her out of her unpleasant musing by speaking her name as though he'd had to repeat it several times. "Yes?" she asked breathlessly. Why was oxygen suddenly so scarce?

"I asked how long you've been Mrs. Robins."

"Oh, uh, seven years. But then I *haven't* been Mrs. Robins for two years."

His brows, which were a trifle shaggy and thoroughly masculine, lifted in silent query.

"It's a long, boring story." She glanced down at the toe of her flat-heeled cordovan shoe. "Dr. Robins and I parted company two years ago. That's when I decided to go back to school."

"But this is an undergraduate course."

Had any other man worn jeans and western boots with a sportcoat he would have looked as though he were imitating a film star, but Grant Chapman looked absolutely devastating. Did it have anything to do with the open throat of his plaid cotton shirt, which revealed a dark wedge of chest hair?

She forced her eyes away from it to answer him. "That's what I am. An undergraduate, I mean." She had no idea how delectable her mouth looked when she smiled naturally. For the last few years smiles hadn't come easily. But when they did, the weariness that had been etched on her face by unhappiness was relieved, and her lips tilted at the corners and were punctuated with shallow dimples.

Grant Chapman seemed intrigued by those indentations at either side of her mouth. It took him a long time to reply. "I would have thought that since you were such a good student, you would have gone to college as soon as you graduated from Poshman Valley."

"I did. I went to the University of Oklahoma, but . . ." She glanced away as she remembered her first semester in Norman and how meeting Daryl Robins had changed the course of her life. "Things happen," she finished lamely.

"How are things in Poshman Valley? I haven't been back since I left. God, that's been . . ."

"Ten years," she supplied immediately and then wanted to bite her tongue. She sounded like a good little girl giving her teacher the correct answer. "Something like that," she added with deliberate casualness.

"Yes, because I went to Washington directly from there. I left before the year was up."

Self-defensively she averted her eyes. The next hour of afternoon classes must have begun. Only a few students drifted by on the sidewalks outside the multipaned windows.

She couldn't talk about his leaving. He wouldn't remember, and she had tried for ten years to forget. "Things in Poshman Valley never change. I get back fairly often to see my folks. They still live there. My brother is teaching math and coaching football at the junior high."

"No kidding!" He laughed.

"Yes. He's married and has two children." She adjusted her armload of heavy books into a more comfortable position against her breasts. When he saw the gesture, he leaned forward to take them from her and set them on the desk behind him. That left her without anything to do with her hands, so she folded them awkwardly across her waist, hoping he wouldn't guess how exposed she felt.

"Do you live here in Cedarwood?"

"Yes. Since I'm going to school full-time, I rented a small house."

"An older one?"

"How did you know?"

"There are a lot of them here. It's a very quaint little town. Reminds me of Georgetown. I lived there the last few years I was in Washington."

"Oh." She felt terribly gauche. He had hob-nobbed with the elite, the beautiful, the powerful. How provincial she must seem to him.

She made a move to retrieve her books. "I don't want to keep you—"

"You're not. I'm finished for the day. As a matter of fact, I was going to get a cup of coffee some-where. Would you join me?"

Her heart pounded furiously. "No, thank you, Mr. Chapman, I—"

His laughter stymied her objection. "Really, Shelley, I think you can call me by my first name. You're not in high school any longer."

"No, but you're still my teacher," she reminded him, slightly perturbed that he had laughed at her.

"And I'm delighted to be. You decorate my classroom. Now more than ever." She wished he had kept laughing. That was easier to handle than his intent scrutiny of her features. "But, please, don't categorize me as a college professor. The word 'professor' conjures up a picture of an absent-minded old man with a headful of wild white hair searching through the pockets of his baggy tweed coat for the eyeglasses perched on top of his head."

She laughed easily. "Maybe you should try teaching creative writing. That was a very graphic word picture you painted."

"Then you get my point. Make it Grant, please."

"I'll try," was all she would promise.

"Try it out."

She felt like a three-year-old about to recite "Mary Had a Little Lamb" for the first time. "Really, I—"

"Try it," he insisted.

"Very well." She sighed. "Grant." The name came more easily to her tongue than she had imagined. In all her fantasies over the past ten years, had she called him by his first name? "Grant, Grant," she repeated.

"See? See how much better that is? Now, how about coffee? You don't have another class do you? Even if you do, you're late, so . . ."

Still she hesitated. "I don't—"

"Unless you'd rather not be seen with me." His change of tone brought her eyes flying up to his. The words had been spoken quietly, but there was a trace of bitterness lying just below the surface.

She caught his meaning instantly. "You mean because of what happened in Washington?" When he answered by silently piercing her with those gray-green eyes, she shook her head vehemently. "No, no, of course not, Mr. . . . Grant. That has nothing to do with it."

She was touched that his relief was so apparent. "Good." He raked strong, lean fingers through his hair. "Let's go for coffee."

Had the look in his eyes and that boyishly vulnerable gesture not compelled her to go with him, the urgency behind his words would have. "All right," she heard herself say before a conscious decision was made.

He smiled, turned to pick up her stack of books and his own folder of notes, and propelled her toward the door. When they reached it, he leaned across her back to switch off the lights. She was aware of his arm resting fleetingly on her back and held her breath.

For an instant, his hand closed around the base of her neck before sliding to the middle of her back. Though the gesture was nothing more than common courtesy, she was acutely aware of his hand through the knit of her sweater as they walked across the campus.

Hal's, that microcosm of society that is on every college campus in the country, was noisy, smoky, crowded. Neil Diamond was lamenting his loneliness from the speakers strategically embedded in the ceiling. Waiters with red satin armbands on their long white sleeves were carrying pitchers of draft beer to cluttered tables. Students of every description, from preppies and sorority girls to bearded intellectuals to muscled jocks, were smelted together in convivial confusion.

Grant took her arm and steered her to a relatively private table in the dim far corner of the tavern. Having secured them their seats, he leaned across the table and said in a stage whisper, "I hope I don't have to show my I.D." At her puzzled frown he explained, "I don't think anyone over thirty would be welcomed in here." Then, at her laughing expression, he clapped his hand to his forehead. "By God, you're not even thirty, are you? Why do suddenly feel more and more like our white-haired doddering professor?"

When the waiter came whizzing by, Grant slowed him long enough to call, "Two coffees."

"Cream?" the fleeing waiter asked over his shoulder.

"Cream?" Grant asked her. She nodded.

"Cream," he shouted to the waiter. "You weren't even old enough to drink coffee the last time I saw you, were you?" he asked her.

Not really listening to his question, she shook her head. She was having a hard time keeping herself from staring at him. His hair was attractively windblown. The open "V" of his shirt continued to bemuse her. Daryl Robins had thought himself the epitome of masculinity, yet his chest had had only a sprinkling of pale hair in the center, while this was a veritable forest growing from darkly tanned skin. An urge to reach out and touch it with her fingertips was so powerful, she looked away.

One glance around the room confirmed what she had suspected. Coeds were eyeing Grant with the unconcealed sexual interest of the modern woman. She was the subject of their cool appraisal. Grant

Chapman was a celebrity in a notorious, dangerous way, with the kind of reputation no woman could resist being curious about. Shelley had tried to ignore the ripple of attention that their arrival had created, but the bold stares being directed toward them now were most disconcerting.

"You get used to it," he said softly after a moment.

"Do you?"

"No, you don't really get *used* to it, you just learn to live with it and ignore it if you can." He twirled a glass ashtray on the highly glazed wooden tabletop. "That's only one consequence of having your face in the news every day for several months. Whether you're the good guy or the bad guy, the culprit or the victim, guilty or innocent, notoriety shadows you. Nothing you do is private anymore."

She didn't say anything until after the harried waiter had served them their coffee. Shelley stirred cream into her cup and said gently, "They'll get accustomed to seeing you around. News that you'd be joining the faculty this fall spread through the campus like wildfire last spring. Once you're here for a while, the excitement will die down."

"My classes filled up quickly. I don't find that flattering. I realize most of the students who registered for them did so out of curiosity. I saw the cowboy sitting next to you sleeping today."

She smiled, glad that he didn't have that intense, guarded expression on his face any longer. "I don't think he appreciated the finer points of your lecture."

Grant returned her smile briefly and then gazed

at her earnestly, searching the depths of her eyes with an intensity that made her quail. "Why did you take my class, Shelley?"

She looked down into her coffee; then, thinking that silence would incriminate her, she said spiritedly, "Because I needed the credit."

He ignored her attempted levity. "Were you a curiosity seeker, too? Did you want to see if I'd grown horns and a long tail since you'd seen me?"

"No," she cried softly. "Of course not. Never."

"Did you want to see if I'd remember you?" He was leaning forward now, his forearms propped against the edge of the table. The distance between them was visibly decreased, but rather than shrinking from him, she felt an irresistible urge to move closer still.

"I . . . I guess I did. I didn't think you would remember. It's been so long and—"

"Did you want to see if I remembered the night we kissed?"

2

Her heart slammed against her ribs. The noise of the room diminished under the thundering pulse in her eardrums. Her mouth went dry.

"Look at me, Shelley."

No, no, don't, Shelley. You'll be lost. He'll see. He'll know. Her eyes disobeyed the frantic order of her brain and lifted to meet his. She saw her reflection in the greenish depths, a shattered expression, a face full of sadness, of perplexity.

"I remember kissing you. Do you remember it?"

She nodded before she spoke. "Yes." Momentarily she closed her eyes as a wave of vertigo seized her. She prayed he'd drop the subject, go on to something neutral that they could discuss openly and easily. She didn't think she'd survive reliving that life-altering night while he sat just inches from her.

The times she had reviewed it privately were innumerable. The memory was locked away in the most secret part of her being, a treasure trove that no one knew about. She had been miserly with that memory, bringing it forth and reliving it only when she was alone. But discussing that night with him would be like undergoing a medical examination. Nothing would be hidden. She couldn't do it.

He was unmerciful. "It was after the championship basketball game. Do you remember?"

"Yes," she answered, forcing a leaden dullness into her voice to keep from screaming. "Poshman Valley won."

"And everyone went crazy," he said softly. "The band must have played the fight song ten times in succession. Everybody in town was there, yelling and screaming. The players were lifting the coach over their heads and parading him around the gym floor."

She could see it all. Hear it all. Smell the popcorn. She could still feel the floor vibrating beneath her feet as everyone stamped in time to the blaring music the band was playing.

"Shelley, go get the victory banner," one of the other cheerleaders had screamed into her ear. She had nodded and fought her way through the rejoicing spectators to the office where the cheerleaders had left the banner.

Shelley had been dashing out the door with it tucked under her arm when Mr. Chapman came running in. He had been sent for the trophy that was to be presented to the victors.

"Mr. Chapman!" Shelley had shrieked excitedly as she rushed toward him.

He was as caught up in the enthusiasm of the victory as anyone. Without thinking, he clasped his arms around her waist, lifted her off the floor, and whirled her round and round, their laughter filling the small confines of the office.

When he set her back on her feet, he paused a moment too long in releasing her. When his arms should have fallen to his sides immediately, he hesitated and they remained locked behind her back. The moment was unpredictable, possibly unfortunate, certainly unplanned. That one heartbeat in time was both her death and her birth. For in that moment, Shelley was forever changed.

Astonishment choked off laughter. Silence, except for the dull roar coming through the walls from the gym, reigned. Their hearts seemed to pulse together. She could feel the pounding of his through her sweater with its stiff felt "PV" appliquéd in the center. The hard muscles of his thighs pressed against her legs, bare beneath her short wool skirt. One of his hands stayed at her waist while the other opened wide and firm over the middle of her back. Their breath intermingled as his face lowered imperceptibly.

They stood frozen, staring at each other in mute wonder. He tilted his head to one side, as though he had just been struck between the eyes and couldn't quite figure out yet what had hit him.

Then swiftly, almost as if just realizing the precariousness of their situation, he ducked his head.

His mouth touched hers, sweetly, sweetly. It lingered. Pressed. It parted her lips. Then the tip of his tongue touched hers. Sizzling electricity jolted through both of them.

He released her with jarring abruptness and stepped away. He saw the mortified tears spring into her frightened eyes and his heart twisted with self-loathing. "Shelley—"

She fled.

The banner was still tucked under her arm when she ran headlong out of the gymnasium to her family's car. When her worried parents found her huddled in the backseat a half hour later, she told them she had become ill and had had to leave.

"I terrified you that night," Grant said now. He didn't touch her, though his hand lay close to hers on the tabletop. If he were to lift his little finger and move it a hair's breadth, he would be touching her.

"Yes, you did." Her voice had deserted her. She could barely croak. "I told my parents I was sick and stayed in bed for three days during Christmas vacation." She tried to smile but found that when she did, her lips trembled.

She had lain in her bed, confused and distressed, wondering why her breasts throbbed each time she remembered the way Mr. Chapman's lips felt against hers. Why, when her boyfriend's anxious groping had never done anything except irritate her, had she longed to feel Mr. Chapman's hands on her everywhere. Stroking. Petting. Closing over her breasts. Touching their crests. Kissing them. She had wept with shame, huge, scalding tears that were absorbed by her pillow.

"You weren't the only one who was terrified. You scared the hell out of me," Grant said quietly. Shelley looked at him in bewilderment. He laughed without humor. "Can you imagine what a community the size of Poshman Valley would have done to a teacher seen kissing one of his students? I would have been lucky to die quickly. Thank God no one saw us that night. For your sake more than mine. I could leave. You couldn't."

"You left right after that." She had dreaded going back to school after that holiday. How would she face him? But she had learned before the first class convened that Mr. Chapman would no longer be teaching at Poshman Valley. He had resigned to accept a post as a congressional aide in Washington, D.C. Everyone had known that he was marking time teaching until he could go to the capital, but everyone was surprised that he had left so suddenly.

"Yes. I went to Oklahoma City over the holiday and pestered my contacts until one of them finally lined me up a job. I couldn't go back to the high school."

"Why?"

He pierced her with his moss-colored eyes. His voice was quiet and intense when he spoke. "You may have been an innocent then, Shelley, but you aren't now. You know why I had to leave. That kiss was far from fraternal. It had never occurred to me to touch you like that, much less to kiss you. Please believe that. I hadn't harbored any lecherous thoughts about you or any student. But once I held you in my arms, something happened. You were no longer a student of mine, but a desirable woman. I doubt I would have ever been able to treat you as a schoolgirl again."

She thought the pressure in her chest might very well kill her. Yet she lived long enough to hear him ask, "Are you finished? More coffee?"

"Yes. I mean yes, I'm finished, and no thank you. No more."

"Let's go."

He stood and held her chair for her. She rose quickly, careful not to touch him.

"Whew," he said, pushing open the heavy, brass-studded door and escorting her outside. "Fresh air."

"Hello, Mr. Chapman."

A coed paused to speak to him as she entered the restaurant with three other girls. Her eyelashes were heavy with mascara; her mouth, glossed with vermilion, was wide and full; her hair was layered and permed to give a tousled effect. Shelley wondered if the girl had been welded into her jeans, for surely no zipper would stand that much strain. Her generous breasts were unconfined by a bra beneath her crocheted sweater.

"Hello, Miss . . ."

"Zimmerman. Monday-Wednesday-Friday, two-o'clock class. I certainly enjoyed your lecture yesterday," she cooed. "I've checked out some of the books you recommended from the library."

"But have you read them?"

The girl blinked dully for a moment, stunned by Grant's derisive question. Then she smiled lazily, deciding to take his jibe with good humor. "I've started them."

"Good. When you're done, I'd like to hear your impressions."

"Oh, you will. You will." Her cunning glance slid over Shelley, who was treated to a chilly evaluation. "See ya," she said as she followed her friends into Hal's.

They had walked half a block down the bookstore-lined sidewalk before Grant said lightly, "No comments?"

"On what?" she asked breezily.

"On the dedication of some students."

She looked up at him scoffingly. "I'm sure Miss Zimmerman is dedicated to many things, but I doubt that scholastics is one of them."

He laughed, taking her arm and leading her across the street. "Where are you parked?"

"I'm not. I walked to campus today."

"Commendable. Which way?"

The safest, wisest, easiest thing to do would be to part company here and now. Shelley Robins always did the safest, wisest, easiest thing. She paused on the sidewalk and faced him. "Thank you, but I can go the rest of the way alone."

"No doubt. But I want to come with you."

"It's not necessary."

"I didn't say it was."

"It's better if you don't."

"Why?"

"Because you're a teacher and I'm your student," she said, dangerously close to tears for reasons she couldn't name.

"As we were before. Is that what's bothering you?"

"I guess so. Yes."

"With one vital difference, Shelley. This time we're both mature adults."

She hedged, gnawing her bottom lip.

Taking advantage of her indecision, he pressed his point. "Believe me, the last thing I need in my life is a scandal. I wouldn't do anything to compromise either of us."

"That's why we shouldn't be seen together off campus at all." His position at the university was shaky at best. Why would he jeopardize it? Along with his problems, she had to analyze what his being in her life again would mean to her.

No. She couldn't become entrapped again. She'd have to bring things to a screeching halt now. Why she had ever let him talk about that kiss ten years ago, she couldn't fathom, but . . .

"I need a friend, Shelley."

Her head snapped up to see the lines engraved on either side of his mouth and the deep furrow between his brows. He had suffered. He had known untold trouble. Had he made a romantic appeal, she would have rebuffed it. Probably. Maybe.

But that simple, pitiable request for friendship couldn't be denied. He was something of a celebrity, yes. But he was also a victim of his own notoriety. Someone of his caliber didn't inspire friendship in ordinary people who lived mundane lives. It was inverted snobbery. The fact of the matter was—he was lonely.

She looked up into the alluring, knowing eyes and saw a hint of insecurity. "All right," she agreed softly and began walking again.

He matched his stride to hers. "What are you majoring in?"

"Banking."

He stopped in his tracks. *"Banking?"*

She stopped, too. "Yes, banking. What did you expect me to say? Home economics?" There was undisguised asperity in her voice. To her surprise, he burst out laughing.

"No. I'm not a chauvinist. It's just that I can't see you as a stodgy banker in a gray pin-striped suit."

"Lord, I hope not," she said, relaxing somewhat. They started walking again. "I want to specialize in banking from the woman's point of view. Many banks now have departments that cater to women, particularly women who have their own businesses or divorcées or widows who for the first time are having to manage their money. Often they don't know the first thing about balancing a checkbook much less opening a savings account or securing a loan."

"You have my wholehearted approval," he said, placing a hand over his heart. "I think it's a great idea."

"Thank you." She dropped a curtsy.

The sidewalks were all but deserted now. The sun had set behind Gresham Hall and the sky was tinted a pale shade of indigo. Oaks and elms, their leaves burnished by the cool fall weather, overhung the sidewalk, lending it intimacy. Indeed one couple had found this romantic aura too difficult to resist.

Grant's and Shelley's footsteps echoed hollowly on the cracked, lichen-covered sidewalk as they approached the couple. The young woman's back was pressed against the trunk of a tree as the young man leaned into her. His feet straddled hers. Their heads were angled, mouths fused. Their arms were wound around each other.

As Shelley guiltily watched them, the man's hips rotated slowly and the woman's hand slipped lower from his waist to apply encouraging pressure. All the blood in her body rushed to Shelley's face and bathed it with a bright stain. She risked looking at Grant out of the corner of her eye and was further embarrassed to see that he was studying her reaction closely. He smiled crookedly and picked up their pace until the oblivious lovers were left far behind.

"Are you working now?" Grant asked, to relieve the tension between them.

"No. I'm a professional student. I decided to devote all my time and effort to my education. I managed to finance it so I wouldn't have to work."

"Cash settlement?"

She never discussed her divorce, but strangely she wasn't offended by Grant's question. The bitterness that had stayed with her for months after the final papers had been signed had gradually abated. Regrets remained, but then she had expected that. "Yes. I didn't want to rely on Daryl for my livelihood, but I felt he owed me an education. We finally came to an agreement that satisfied both of us."

"Would you mind if I asked what happened?"

"We got married mistakenly and got divorced five years later."

They crossed another deserted street before he said, "No details?"

She looked up at him. "Please."

"I'm sorry. I didn't mean to pry. It's just that I think the man's a damned fool, and if I ever meet him face-to-face, I'm likely to tell him so."

"It doesn't matter. He has what he wants. He's a doctor in Oklahoma City, outstanding in his field. When last I heard, he was squiring the chief of staff's daughter. Daryl would consider that a real feather in his cap."

Grant breathed an expletive through firmly set lips. "I guess you sacrificed your education to work and put him through medical school."

"Something like that, yes." She was alarmed at the fierceness of his expression. "Here's my house," she said nervously.

He followed her up the narrow, somewhat uneven sidewalk to the alcove that sheltered the arched front door. The house was made of dark reddish-brown brick and trimmed with white woodwork. The grass and shrubbery were well clipped, but the yard was littered with fallen leaves from the twin pecan trees on either side of the center sidewalk.

"I love it, Shelley," Grant said enthusiastically.

"Do you? I did, too, from the moment I saw it. I'll hate to part with it when I graduate and leave."

"And where will you go? Do you have any prospects for a job?"

"Not just now, but this spring I'll start sending out letters of inquiry. I suppose I'll have to gravitate toward the metropolitan areas in order to find a bank large enough to support a separate women's department."

By the end of her speech, her voice was no more than a slender thread of sound. It unnerved her for him to be watching her mouth with that devouring look.

"Thank you for—" she began.

"Shelley, aren't you the least bit curious? You haven't asked why a beautiful, rich senator's daughter would kill herself over me."

She was dumbfounded. Never had she expected him to bring up the subject of his expulsion from Washington so openly. Of course she had been curious. The entire country had been. When the headlines came off the press proclaiming the suicide of one of Washington's darlings, the public had been outraged.

For month's prior to her death Missy Lancaster had been keeping close company with Grant Chapman. Senator Lancaster of Oklahoma had seemed to endorse what everyone believed to be a budding romance. When the young woman was found dead from an overdose of sleeping pills in her Georgetown apartment, the bubble of enchantment surrounding them had burst. Grant Chapman was circumstantially implicated; it was believed that he had broken her heart and he was fired from the senator's staff.

Chapman had then had the bad grace to file a breach-of-contract suit against Senator Lancaster. The news services had had a field day. What could be better than a nude girl, found lying dead in her bed with a note written in her own hand? It had read, "My dearest darling, forgive me for loving you too well. If I can't have you, then I want to die." To make matters worse, the autopsy had revealed that Missy Lancaster was pregnant. The public fed on each sordid detail voraciously.

Grant had won his suit, but had resigned his post immediately after the judge handed down his ruling. Grant Chapman might have been dubbed insensitive, but no one had ever accused him of being stupid. He was smart enough to know that in Washington he would forever be ostracized.

"I . . . I felt sorry for you, having to go through something like that," she said at last.

He laughed harshly. "You must have been the only one in the country who sympathized with *me*, the dastardly villain of the piece. Didn't you for one minute think that all the things they said about me might be true? Didn't you ever believe I was a despoiler of virgins? Or wonder if it was my baby that died in the womb of his suicidal mother?" Under the anger of his demanding questions, she took a step backward and he knew instant remorse. He raked a hand through his hair and sighed heavily. For a moment he stared down at the brick porch beneath his boots. "I'm sorry, Shelley."

"Don't apologize. You've every right to be bitter.

Whatever happened between you and Missy Lancaster, you ended up the one being victimized."

He attempted a wry smile. "Where were you when I needed you? I could have used you in my corner cheering me on."

"Things will work out. People will forget."

"Will *you?*" He set her books on the ledge bordering the porch and took a step closer to her.

"Will . . . will I what?"

"Will you forget that I was involved in a scandal concerning a young girl when you know that ten years ago I kissed one much younger?"

If only there were some motion, some sound to alleviate the ponderous stillness around them. Without distractions, all her senses were concentrated on him. He filled her field of vision with his height and breadth of shoulder. She could smell the woodsy fragrance of his cologne, hear the sound of his heartbeat.

"What happened in Poshman Valley was an accident," she rasped.

"Was it?" he asked softly. "For a long time afterward I told myself it was, but seeing you the other day, I had to face up to the fact that maybe it wasn't. Maybe I wasn't as detached as I knew I should be. Maybe I saw in you then the promise of the woman you are now. Shelley—"

"No." When he took one step nearer, she backed away. "No, Grant."

"Why?"

"*Why?* Because the circumstances are still the same."

"That's no reason, Shelley. How old are you?

Twenty-six? Twenty-seven? I'm thirty-five. If I were anyone else and we met at a cocktail party, you'd never give our ages a thought."

She wrung her hands in an effort to still their trembling. Or was it to keep from touching him? To keep from brushing that lock of silvered hair off his brow? To keep from laying her hand flat on his lapel? "It's not age; it's status. I'm still your student."

"At Poshman Valley High School that mattered. Not here. Not in this day and age. I think we owe it to ourselves and to each other to see if that kiss of ten years ago was just a fluke. Or the harbinger of something more." He came to her and laid his strong hands on her shoulders.

"Don't, please. Don't say any more."

"Listen to me," he said urgently, backing her against the wall. "You were like a breath of fresh air when you walked through that classroom door the other day. After the quagmire my life has been, you were a reminder of happier days. I'd never forgotten that December night, but the impact of it had dimmed. Seeing you again was a very forcible reminder and it brought back all the ambivalence I felt ten years ago.

"I want to kiss you again, Shelley. My career is blown to hell. I've seen how fleeting success and happiness are. So what if someone disapproves of us? I'm tired of trying to please other people. The payoff's not so good. I'm going to kiss you, Shelley. I've got absolutely nothing to lose."

He trapped her jaw between his thumb and fingers, cradling the underside of it in his palm. Her hands came up to fend him off, but ended up clutching his shoulders. For a long moment, he stared down into her wide, apprehensive eyes, then he lowered his head.

His lips were warm, firm, confident, but soft. They slanted over her mouth, moving in such a way that she never knew the precise instant her lips opened to the light pressure of his tongue. She heard a whimper of satisfaction as he took complete possession, but didn't realize that she had made the sound.

His tongue rubbed along hers, mating with it, exploring her with meticulous care. He tickled the roof of her mouth with the tip of his tongue, dragged it along her teeth, penetrated as far as he could to leave nothing undiscovered.

The manacles of ten years of depression dropped from her limbs. Her hands went to the back of his neck to touch the dark strands that brushed his collar. Ten years of longing, of fantasies, went into the kiss. Her heart expanded to the bursting point with a rush of pent-up emotion.

He sipped at the moisture shining on her lower lip. "Shelley, Shelley, my God," he whispered against her mouth. His tongue delved into the sweet vault again, greedier this time. It was met with equal fervor.

He released her jaw, lowered his arm and encircled her waist. The other hand slid down her spine to the small of her back, pressing, urging her closer. With such an intimate positioning of their bodies, she knew at once the hard evidence of his maleness and was shocked.

The feel of it startled her back into consciousness. The stark reality of their situation broke through the passion that had robbed her of rational thought. She pushed against his chest and jerked her head backward.

"Let me go, please," she said in panic.

He released her immediately and took a step backward to give her the space she obviously needed. Her fingers were shaking as she massaged her forehead with them. The tortured expression on her face and the agitated way she shook her head plainly indicated her distress.

"Thank you for walking me home. I have to go in now." She turned, but was caught by his hand clasping her upper arm.

"Shelley, please don't run from me again."

"I'm not running." She avoided his eyes. "I have a lot to—"

"You're running," he interrupted. "I couldn't pursue you before, but I won't let you go this time without an explanation. Did I come on too strong, too fast? Are you still in love with your husband?"

She laughed then, but it was an ugly sound. Unhealthy mirth. "No. I assure you that is not the case."

"Then what?"

She looked at him, defeated and dispirited, her shoulders slumping. "Grant," she whispered half angrily, "you know why we can't . . . why this must never happen again. I started thinking of you as my teacher the first time I walked into your classroom ten years ago. In the course of a few hours I can't change the image I formed of you then. In my mind you're still off limits to me. And whether you want to admit it or not, I am to you."

His eyes fell away from hers to her mouth, then to her shoulder. His reluctance to hold her gaze told her he knew she was right. He relinquished her arm and shoved his hands into his pockets.

"You have a chance now to make a new career for yourself. This," she said, sawing her hand back and forth between them to indicate the entire situation, "isn't worth risking your reputation."

His eyes swung back to hers. "I'll decide that."

"I've already decided. We can't let this go any further. It would spell disaster for both of us. It just isn't right. It wasn't then, and it isn't now."

Before he could say another word, she had unlocked her door and whirled inside, slamming it shut behind her. She leaned against the door for a long time, until she heard his slow, dejected footsteps fade down the sidewalk.

The tears that had threatened for so long were finally permitted to fall.

3

"You look wonderful, Shelley," she muttered to the tear-swollen face in the mirror over her bathroom sink. She dabbed at her red-rimmed eyes with a tissue and leaned over to rinse her face again with cold water. When she dried it, she pressed the velour towel against her eyes, hoping to block out the ever-present image of Grant Chapman.

If you haven't been able to do that in ten years, what makes you think you can do it now? she asked herself. He was more charismatic, more handsome, and to her discerning woman's eye, more virile than he had ever been before. As the object of an adolescent infatuation, he had posed a threat to her well-being, but not half the threat he posed now.

The man she'd never been able to forget had

stepped back into her life and she didn't know how she was going to cope with that. As she poured cereal and milk into a bowl she chastised herself for enrolling in his class. There were seven thousand students at the university. The chances of their running into each other would have been slim. Yet she had purposely made it necessary for them to see each other at least twice a week.

Her supper snapped, crackled and popped, but she didn't taste any of it as she chewed mechanically. She had cooked very little since her divorce; as a result she had shed the twelve pounds that had crept up on her during her five years of marriage. Once the divorce was final, she had sworn never to cook a meal for a man again. For no matter what time Daryl came home from the hospital, he had expected her to have a hot meal on the table waiting for him.

Disdain for the obedient servant she had become was like a bad taste in her mouth. Angrily she rinsed her bowl out in the sink, washing half of the cereal into the garbage disposal. "Never again," she vowed.

She had met Daryl Robins at a sorority rush party her first week at O.U. She was straight out of Poshman Valley, and to her a good-looking premed student was the height of romance.

After their first dance, they didn't switch partners the rest of the night. The way he held her during the slow dances made her nervous, but after all she was a college girl now. Besides, he wasn't overly aggressive. His dimpled smile and blond handsomeness were heart-melting in their guilelessness.

He pinned her on Homecoming weekend. By Christmas their dates had become little more than skirmishes. "For godsake, Shelley, will you grow up?" he hissed at her from across the backseat of his car. "I'm going to be a doctor. I know how to keep you from getting pregnant if that's what's worrying you."

"It's not that," she sobbed. "I don't think a woman should until—"

"She's married," he mocked. His crude expletive indicated the depth of his frustration. "Where have you been living? In the twilight zone?"

"Don't make fun of me or my convictions," she said, showing a flare of spirit. "I can't help feeling the way I do."

He cursed again and stared out the window for a long time. "Hell," he sighed at last. "Do you want to get married? If I ask my dad, he'll help us with money."

Shelley didn't even care that the proposal wasn't exactly poetic. She catapulted herself across the car and threw her arms around his neck. "Oh, Daryl, Daryl."

That night she let him take off her bra and kiss her breasts. He had been delighted; she, disappointed. It didn't feel as good as she had expected it to. But then it wasn't the man she had always imagined. . . .

And now that man was back in her life and she was no better equipped emotionally to handle her feelings for him than she'd ever been. Except she was older and presumably wiser now. Or was she? She knew the wise thing to do would be to drop

Grant Chapman's class; she also knew she wouldn't.

After weighing her decision for hours, wasting time she should have used for studying by staring into space, wondering how she would fend off his attempts to see her alone again, she knew a keen disappointment when he didn't try to contact her at all.

Her heart had been hammering in her chest when she opened the door to the classroom the next time it convened, but she had arrived ahead of him. She took her seat near the back of the room and jumped each time the door opened until Grant blustered through it, his hair windblown, his expression beleaguered. "Sorry, I'm late, everyone," he apologized as he dropped his notes and texts onto the desk.

He didn't speak to her as she left. Relief and aggravation warred within her. She told herself she should be glad he had come to his senses and converted to her way of thinking. Why then was she ruled by a feeling of discontent?

She didn't see him on campus, but at the next meeting of her class he treated her with the same detachment. Only as she passed his desk on her way out did he say a cool, "Hello, Mrs. Robins." To which she replied with an even cooler, "Mr. Chapman."

"Damn him!" she cursed as she threw her pile of heavy textbooks onto her kitchen table. Kicking off her shoes, she went to the refrigerator and yanked open the door. "He's doing it to me again."

In reality, he wasn't doing anything and that was what rankled. "I didn't concentrate on anything but him my whole junior year in high school. He ruined it for me." Of course it hadn't been his fault that she'd had an asinine crush on him then, any more than it was his fault now. The bottles and jars in the refrigerator rattled when she slammed its door closed.

"He won't disrupt my life a second time. He won't!" she said, ripping off the tab on the top of a soda can. Along with it, she ripped off the tip of a fingernail. She covered her face, weeping and cursing in anguish. "I'll get him out of my system if it's the last thing I ever do. I swear I will."

That resolution lasted for all of two days. Laden with assignments and reading lists, she trudged up the marble steps of the library, determined to devote single-minded attention to her studies.

Grant Chapman was the first person she saw as she entered the austere building.

He was sitting at a long table with a group of faculty members from the political-science department. He didn't see her, so she took the opportunity to study him with a fascination that had never diminished.

In spite of the silver in the hair at his temples, he looked more like a student than a teacher. He was wearing a casual pair of tan slacks and a navy pullover, V-necked sweater. The sleeves had been pushed to his elbows. His chin was resting on his fists as he leaned over the table to hear what one of his colleagues was saying.

Grant offered a comment and everyone laughed softly, especially the woman sitting next to him. She appeared to be in her mid-thirties and was attractive in a bespeckled, bookish sort of way. Grant smiled back at her.

"Hiya, Shelley."

She whirled around to face a young man who was in her economics class. "Hi, Graham. How's the reading?"

"Boring," he said as he passed her on his way to the exit.

Calling a soft good-bye to him, she was still smiling when she turned around. Her smile froze when her eyes collided with Grant's. He was staring at her from under lowered brows, paying little or no attention to the professor who was speaking earnestly to the others. He defied her to ignore him, so she merely nodded her head once in greeting and turned on the heel of her loafer toward the stairs.

She found an empty table in a deserted corner of the third-floor stacks and spread out the mound of books she had to read. Graham was right. The material was boring at best. A half hour later, the words were blurring before her eyes and running together meaninglessly.

To occupy her wandering mind, she tracked the approaching footsteps that tapped lightly on the tile floor. Walk, walk, stop. Turn. Go back. Forward. Stop. Walk, walk . . .

Suddenly he was standing in front of her at the end of a long canyon formed by towering bookshelves. A smile of gratification tugged at the corners of his mouth. Had he been looking for her?

Quickly she lowered her eyes to the text in front of her. In her peripheral vision, she saw his trousered legs coming closer until he stood directly in front of her across the narrow table. When he set down a folder stuffed with papers, she raised her eyes to his, then glanced pointedly at an unoccupied table a few feet away.

"Is this seat taken?" he asked with exaggerated politeness, bowing slightly at the waist.

"No. And neither is that one." She indicated the other table with a nod of her head.

He gave it only a cursory look over his shoulder. "The lighting is better over here." He tried to pull the chair out, but met resistance. Bending down to see what was keeping it from sliding out from under the table, he chuckled softly. "This chair *is* taken." Her stockinged feet were propped on it.

She lowered them to the floor and he sat down. Why had she pretended to be annoyed by his intrusion? Actually, her heart was jumping with glee that he had sought her out. If the depth of feeling she saw in his eyes was any indication, he was just as glad to be alone with her. For long, silent moments, they stared at each other. Then, fighting the need to reach out and touch him, she lowered her head back to her book and feigned interest.

"Here," he said, patting his thigh under the table.

"What?" she asked breathlessly, bringing her head back up. She ought to act as though she were engrossed in her studies, as though he had interrupted her. Why didn't she gather up her things and leave?

"Put your feet in my lap."

Her heart pounded wildly. "No," she said in a whisper, glancing over her shoulder.

"There's no one around," he said, and she was drawn under the bewitching spell of his low voice. "Please. Aren't they cold?"

She wouldn't admit they were. "You shouldn't have left your meeting," she said, hoping to change the direction of the conversation.

"It was over."

"I'm sure you have something else to do."

"I do," he said, opening the folder and smiling benignly. "I have some reading to catch up on. Now come on, lift your feet up."

"Grant . . . Mr. Chapman . . . I can't sit here with my feet in your lap. What if someone saw us?"

His grin faded a trifle and he weighed her words. "Does it matter to you that much? What people think of you?"

It wasn't a casual question and she didn't treat it as such. She faltered, lowering her eyes from the penetrating power of his. "Yes. Perhaps it shouldn't, but it does. Doesn't it matter to you what people think?" She looked up at him again.

He considered her question. "No," he answered softly, but with conviction. "Maybe I should pay more attention to the opinions of other people. It might be safer, more judicious. But I could waste a lot of valuable time guessing at what someone thought of me, and then I'd probably be wrong. In the long run, it's better to do what you feel is right for you than to do what you think others feel is right for you. Within the limits of decency and the law, of course." He smiled, but she wasn't ready to dismiss his philosophy without more discussion. She wanted so badly to understand him.

"Is that how you were able to bounce back after the Washington scandal? If something like that had happened to me, I'd want to sequester myself and never come out. Whether I was guilty or innocent, if everyone thought I was guilty, I'd never want to face the world again. You joke, you laugh," she said, remembering the jest he'd made to his colleagues just that evening. "I don't think I'd be able to laugh for a long while if something like that happened to me."

He smiled gently. "I'm a fighter, Shelley. Always have been. I didn't do anything wrong and I'll be damned before I'll let erroneous public opinion keep me from living as happy and full a life as possible." He reached across the table and took her hand. It never occurred to her to pull away. "Frankly," he said with chagrin, "there were times when if I hadn't laughed, I would have cried."

Later, she didn't recall ever lifting her legs and letting him secure her feet between his thighs. But at some point she became aware of him pressing the hard muscles of his thighs against them and massaging the soles with his thumbs.

"I guessed right. They're cold," he whispered.

Why was he whispering? Minutes had ticked by and they hadn't said a word, gazing at each other over the ink-stained table piled with neglected papers. No one had invaded their privacy. The dim halls of the library were hushed. The tall shelves of dusty volumes formed a stockade around them. He whispered because even though they were in a public building, the moment was intimate and belonged exclusively to them.

"It's chilly in here," she murmured, mindless of what she was saying. It didn't matter. She was speaking to him. He was so close to her she could count the fine lines that edged his eyes, hear his faintest whisper. For years she had yearned for the sight of him. Now she gluttonously feasted on it.

"You could put your sweater on." The sleeves of a cardigan were knotted around her neck.

She shook her head. "I'm fine." Actually she was becoming uncomfortably warm. Her head felt incredibly heavy and as light as a bubble at one and the same time. She was somnambulant, but aware of every tingling sensation in her body.

She hadn't experienced this conflict of emotions since the days when she had sat in his classroom at Poshman Valley and graded papers while he worked nearby. One moment she had wanted to dance, to express the excitement that surged through her. The next she had wanted to surrender to blissful lassitude, to lie down and be blanketed by his weight. She felt that same way now.

For a while they read—or pretended to read. Shelley could only vouch for herself, but she thought Grant might be having as hard a time concentrating on the printed words in front of him as she was. He continued to massage her feet. No longer systematic, his movements were idle, somehow sexual. When he had to turn a page in his book, he held both her feet in one hand until he could return the other one.

She loved to watch his eyes as they traveled across the page. Imagining them moving over her body that way caused her to blush hotly. He raised his head and looked at her inquiringly, smiling slightly at the intent way she was studying him and the warm color mounting in her cheeks.

"It just occurred to me that I don't know anything about you," she blurted out. "Your home, your family. You weren't from Poshman Valley."

"I grew up in Tulsa. I was the second of three sons. My father died while I was in college. I had a very normal, happy childhood. I guess being the middle child accounts for my fighter instincts and the knack I have for getting into trouble. Maybe I'm still only trying to attract attention."

She smiled. "I was the older child and always having to set a good example. Where are your brothers now? And your mother?"

"I lost my youngest brother in the Vietnam war. Mother, whose heart wasn't all that strong, died within months of him."

"I'm sorry," she said, meaning it. She'd never lost anyone in her immediate family. Though she'd been away from home for years, she knew her parents were there, should she need them. The only time she'd disappointed them was with the divorce. It had distressed them greatly; they never had been able to understand the need for it. She hadn't told them that at the time she'd had no choice. Daryl had filed the papers before he saw fit to discuss the divorce with her.

"My older brother lives in Tulsa with his wife and children. I think he's embarrassed by me," he admitted sadly. "I stopped to see them before coming here from Washington. He was friendly and loving enough, but there was an undeniable restraint there."

"Maybe he's only in awe of you."

"Maybe." Grant sighed. "Since there are only the two of us left, I'd like for us to be closer than we are." His eyes scanned her face intently. "I guess it'll be up to his sons to carry on the family name."

She swallowed and glanced down at the page of the periodical she was supposed to be studying. It was filled with line after line of print that she should have digested by now. "It's funny that you . . . that you never married."

"Is it?"

Her head came up. "Isn't it?" Why was her voice tremulous? She cleared her throat.

He shook his head. "Not really. During the first few years in Washington I was too busy with my career to become seriously involved with anyone."

Involved, just not seriously involved, she thought.

"Then, I don't know," he said with a shrug. "I just didn't meet anyone who appealed to me, at least not enough to marry."

The silence that descended was palpable. One could sense the tension between them. His thumbs massaged the arches of her feet with long, slow strokes. With each lazy pass, her throat constricted a degree tighter and the tautening of her breasts became more pronounced.

"Shelley," he said compellingly, and she had no choice but to obey his unspoken command and look at him. "Before the night I kissed you, I never gave a thought to what you and that jock boyfriend of yours did in his souped-up car. But long after I moved to Washington, my imagination drove me close to insanity. I envisioned him ravaging you with kisses, pawing your breasts—"

"Grant, don't." She clamped her upper teeth over her bottom lip.

"For months I tried to convince myself that I was concerned about your virtue, that I had a paternal compulsion to protect it. But then I had to admit why I was so tormented by such thoughts. I was jealous of him. I—"

"No, no. You shouldn't be saying this to me. Don't—"

"I wanted to be the one kissing you, fondling you. I wanted to see your breasts, touch them, kiss—"

"Stop!" she cried, pulling her feet free from his hands and standing up so rapidly she swayed dizzily. "I . . . I need to get another book," she said, almost upsetting her chair as she pushed it back.

Forgetting to put on her shoes, she all but ran from the table and disappeared between the bookshelves. Finding a dark aisle where an overhead fluorescent tube had burned out, she leaned weakly against the cold metal bookshelf, placing her forehead on her folded hands.

"This can't happen to me again," she moaned under her breath. "I can't let *him* happen to me again."

But he'd already physically and emotionally affected her. He had paralyzed her mind so she couldn't think of anything but him. Her body longed for his. She knew from the promising kiss on her front porch that he could satisfy this burning need inside her.

She ached to know fulfillment, held as she was in a prison of desire. Would that his hands, his lips, could give her deliverance. But that wasn't possible. She had fought this yearning for him for years and she would keep on fighting it.

Yet, when he came to her out of the shadows she didn't move.

Motionless, she maintained her leaning position against the shelf when she heard him behind her. She knew the prudent thing to do would be to run as far and as fast as she could, but she didn't move. Instead she stood rooted to the spot, terrified that he would touch her . . . and praying that he would not leave without doing so.

He swept her hair aside with a solicitous hand and placed his lips directly against her ear. "Shelley, what's wrong?"

He molded the contours of his body to hers. He was inches taller, but it was amazing how well they fit together, how his shoulders curved around hers, how his chest protected her back, how his hardness was cushioned against her softness.

"Shelley?" he repeated.

"Everything. Everything is wrong," she said with a mournful shake of her head.

"It's not. I won't let it be wrong. No one will tell me it's wrong. Not this time." His arms came around her waist, hugging her closer.

She shuddered with desire. "Oh, Grant, please don't. I'm not a child any longer."

"Thank God."

"But I'm behaving like one."

"Only if you refuse to recognize and accept what's inevitable between us."

"It's not inevitable. We're mature adults, responsible and accountable for what we do. We should stop this before it gets out of hand. *I* should stop this."

"Can you? Can you stop it, Shelley?"

"Yes, yes, yes," she repeated, but only to keep from saying the opposite.

"I couldn't help kissing you ten years ago. Thank God I was able to restrain myself from pursuing you then. But those restrictions no longer apply. We couldn't nurture the attraction between us then, but we can now. I want to. So do you."

"No," she denied, then gasped when his hands slid up her sides. "No, please, Grant, don't touch me there." But it was too late. His hands closed around her breasts. His lips were at her cheek, emitting hot, unsteady gusts of air. His chest was a bellows expanding and collapsing against her back.

Belying every protest she had made, she flung her head back against his chest and covered his hands with her own. He kneaded her gently. "Harder, harder," she begged with a desperation that, when recalled, would cause her to cringe with mortification. But at the moment all her actions were governed by her senses and their clamoring need for him. Frantically her mouth sought his over her shoulder as the pressure of his caress, under the urging of her hands, increased.

With remarkable discipline, he freed his mouth and turned her in his arms. His fingers interlaced with hers and he positioned their hands on either side of her head as he moved forward to trap her between himself and the bookshelf. She was a willing captive, meeting the smoldering glow of his eyes with her own.

For heart-racing, thunderous moments they only looked at each other. Desire, savage and primitive, crackled between them. Their raspy breathing echoed in the empty stacks.

When he finally lowered his mouth to hers, her lips were parted and waiting. He whispered her name a heartbeat before their mouths came together. He stroked the lining of her mouth delicately with his tongue, and matched the movement with his fingertips on her opened palms.

Giving in to an irresistible urge, he lifted his mouth free of hers and kissed her palms, imitating the way he had kissed her mouth in the soft, receptive center of each. She inclined her head to the side as he administered the erotic caress and moved her lips and nose through the unruly thickness of his dark hair. His tongue probed the sensitized hollow of each hand until she was near sobbing with want of him.

Kissing her lips again, he rocked from side to side, rubbing his chest across her breasts. The nipples hardened instantly, revealing her desire to him.

"Yes, yes," he whispered. Gradually he pulled back to see her better.

He unknotted the sleeves of her sweater from around her neck and moved them aside. With agonizing slowness, his hands combed down her chest to her breasts until they covered them completely. Her nipples tingled in the heat of his palms. Moving his hands to the sides of her breasts, he pushed them together and leaned down to bury his face in the fragrant softness of her cleavage. He breathed deeply, as if her scent were his life-force.

"I want to see you without anything on," he said, standing straight once again. "I know you look beautiful naked. You feel . . . beautiful." When his idly circling thumbs coaxed a higher level of response from the crests of her full breasts, he repeated, "Beautiful."

He eased her away from the shelf, kissing her with drugging passion. His hands slid into the back pockets of her jeans and squeezed her bottom, drawing her ever closer to his hard virility.

"Put your hands under my sweater."

Sliding her hands up from his waist to the middle of his back, she splayed them over the hard, smooth muscles. "You're warm." The words were caught by his open mouth. His tongue flicked at the corners of her lips and over her dimples.

"Touch my front."

She hesitated only an instant before moving one hand around to his chest. With tentative movements encouraged by his ardent kiss, she explored the hair-dusted skin of his stomach and chest. His breath hissed through his lips.

"I want to be inside you," he said on an agonized sigh. "Deep. Surrounded by you."

She answered his sigh, tangling her fingers in the thatch of hair whorling around his navel, and meeting the fervency of his kiss. Provocatively he moved against her and she reciprocated.

At first she thought the blinking lights were only a product of her fevered imagination. Simultaneously they realized that it was the signal the library would be closing within five minutes.

Shakily, breathlessly, they backed away from each other. He captured the hand beneath his sweater and massaged the back of it as he pressed it over his skin. When he extracted it, he brought it to his mouth and kissed each fingertip.

"We'd better go," she said hesitantly when the lights blinked again.

Hastily they went back to their table. She slipped on her shoes while gathering up her study materials. They hurried down the two flights of stairs. They were laughing at their exertion when they reached the lower floor.

"Mr. Chapman, I see you almost got locked in . . ."

The woman's voice trailed off as she saw Shelley beside Grant. Shelley recognized her as the woman who had attended the political-science department meeting with Grant, the one who had laughed at his small joke, the one who didn't seem able to tear her eyes away from him.

She took in their flushed expressions, their dishevelment. No doubt obvious, too, were Shelley's pouting, well-kissed lips, where she felt the wonderful sting of whisker burns. The professor's smiling expression puckered into one of prim censure.

"Good night," Grant said hastily and propelled Shelley by the elbow toward the door that an attendant was waiting to lock.

"Good night, Mr. Chapman," the woman said in an accusatory tone.

Shelley wished the ground would suddenly open up and swallow her. Confused by the sensual excitement of the moment, she had temporarily allowed herself to forget what a relationship between them would look like to anyone else. Now, as she was sent crashing back down to earth it all came back. Such a liaison was out of the question. She would look cheap. People would see her as a new plaything for the errant professor. He would be shunned by disapproving colleagues.

As soon as they gained the parking lot in front of the building she set off toward her car. "Good night, Grant," she said, pulling her arm free.

"Shelley . . . ? Wait a minute," he called after her retreating figure. He grasped her arm and spun her around. "What's the matter now?"

"Nothing," she said, wrenching her arm from his fingers.

"Like hell there's not." He advanced far enough ahead of her to block her path. "Tell me what happened between the third floor and the do—Oh, Miss Elliot saw us together. Is that what you're worried about?"

"Did you see the look on her face? She looked at me like . . . Never mind. Good night." She tried to pass him. He wouldn't let her.

"What do you care what she thinks? Is her opinion all that important?"

She rubbed her forehead wearily. It had begun to pound. "No, not her specifically. Everybody. You're my teacher—"

He jerked her erect, his hands gripping her shoulders. "I'm a man first, dammit. And you're a woman first, before you're anything else. Besides, I don't think that's the real problem, is it? What other roadblocks have you constructed in your mind?"

His perceptiveness frightened her and she stiffened in fear and anger. "Let me go." The manner in which she gave the order brooked no argument and his hands slowly relaxed, then dropped to his sides.

"I'm sorry," he said, glancing around.

She saw the unconscious gesture that revealed so much. "You see, Grant. You're wary, too. Wary of what people will think and say about you if they see us as a couple."

"All right," he said grudgingly. "I'll admit to a little caution. I'd be a fool not to be concerned about my reputation being lambasted again. But it won't be, Shelley. If we're open and aboveboard, who's going to accuse us of anything unseemly?"

She responded to his words with a negative shake of her head. "It doesn't work that way. People are always looking for the worst in others. That's human nature."

"You're avoiding the real issue, aren't you?" he demanded with alarming insight. "What's really troubling you, Shelley?"

"Nothing," she insisted in a strangled tone. "I

have to go." She walked around him, going straight to her car and unlocking the door. She maintained her rigid posture until she drove past him, then she slumped back in the seat.

He was right. He posed problems in her life he couldn't even guess at. And she didn't know how she was going to deal with any of them.

4

Why weren't you in class today? Are you sick?"

It had been two days since she'd seen Grant in the library. The last thing she'd expected was to find him on her doorstep. "No. I'm not sick."

"Why weren't you in class?"

"Do you personally call on all your students who cut class, Mr. Chapman? Doesn't that take up a lot of your valuable time?"

He looked thoroughly annoyed. Putting his hands on his hips, he shifted his weight to one leg. His eyes, under the thick brows, took a long, slow, scornful survey of her. "You're a coward."

"You're right."

Her quick agreement surprised him. He had expected an angry outburst of denial. His exasperation manifested itself in a long sigh. "May I come in?"

"No."

"Yes." He backed her into the room until he could close the door behind him. She sputtered a protest, but he silenced it. "I don't think you want to thrash this out while standing on your front porch."

She glared at him before turning her back to go stand at the window. "Say what you have to say. It will make no difference. I've dropped your class."

"Why?"

"I have too heavy a load this semester," she said, still keeping her back to him.

"Try again."

She pivoted to face him. "Okay," she shouted. No longer the infatuated student in awe of him, she was a woman meeting an adversary on equal footing. "I can't stay in your class after what happened the other night. I should never have let you kiss me."

"You didn't *let* me kiss you. You were doing your fair share."

"I . . . I was . . . To satisfy my curiosity. That's all." She was lying, buying time, and he knew it.

"What did your fancy doctor-husband do to you to make you afraid of sex?"

"I'm not!"

"You're afraid of something."

"You're wrong."

"Then why are you standing there so tense and rigid? Surely you know I would never hurt you.

What did Daryl Robins do to you to make you so guarded around men?"

"Nothing!"

"Tell me!"

"He taught me what heartless, self-serving, selfish creatures they are!" she yelled, her breasts heaving in agitation.

His head went up and back as if she'd clipped him under the chin with a right hook. There were several moments of charged silence.

Now that she'd dropped her bomb, Shelley took a deep breath and continued. "His father didn't come through as Daryl had hoped. In order to support us, I had to quit school and go to work. I worked in an office with a hundred others just like me. I started as a file clerk and gradually worked my way up to the typing pool. For five years I spent eight back-breaking hours a day pounding on that machine.

"When I got home from work I did the shopping, the housework, the laundry, the cooking. Then I typed Daryl's reports. All through his last two years of premed, three years of med school, and one year of residency, I never complained. I was doing my wifely duty. Never mind that I was becoming boring as hell because all I had to talk about was the gossip in the office.

"Daryl worked, too. He studied. I'll give him that much credit. It paid off. He was put on staff at one of the major hospitals in the city."

She paused, taking in another gulp of air. "One night I cooked beef stroganoff, one of his favorites.

He came in, sat down to dinner and said, 'Shelley, I don't love you anymore. I want a divorce.' 'Why?' I cried. 'Because I've outgrown you. We have nothing in common anymore.'

"Now, can you see why I don't want any hassles in my life? I won't be some man's unsalaried housekeeper and bedmate. I'm a free and independent agent. I don't want entanglements or disruptions. Even if you weren't who you are, even if it weren't already impossible that we become involved, I wouldn't want you in my life."

Exhausted, she collapsed into a chair, rested her head on the back cushion and closed her eyes. The woeful tale of her marriage had never been revealed even to her parents. Why she had blurted out the cold hard facts to Grant, she didn't know. But now maybe he'd understand why she refused to see him on any terms.

The only element she had left out of her story was her sexual relationship with Daryl. In five years, it had never improved after a nightmarish wedding night. She had finally learned to tolerate his sweaty, vigorous lovemaking. Through a kind of self-hypnosis, she had trained her body to accept him even though her mind rejected him. Nothing he did stirred her. She lay beneath him as one dead.

Admittedly she had been unfair to Daryl. She had married him for all the wrong reasons. At that time in her life she had believed womanhood and marriage were one and the same. Every woman got married. It was the only truly accepted thing to do. Conforming to other people's standards had been a way of life to Shelley Browning and it never entered her mind to buck the system.

She might have been able to make Daryl happy, and vice-versa, but for the one essential ingredient lacking in their marriage. She didn't love him and never had. Still carrying a secret torch that nonetheless burned brightly and continually in her heart, she had settled for someone else because the man she wanted was out of her reach.

"Shelley." His quiet voice, coming to her from across the room, across the years, was like a caress. In self-protection, she didn't open her eyes. "I'm sorry for the unhappiness you've known. I don't want to be a disruption in your life."

She wanted to scream that he'd always been a disruption. Instead she opened her eyes and said wearily, "Then you won't pursue this relationship?"

He shook his head sadly. "I can't let you slip through my fingers again. I thought if I could see you in class every other day, it might be enough until the semester was over. But after what happened the other night, I know I can't wait any longer. We were off limits to each other before. Not now."

"Yes now. More than ever. Too much has happened to both of us."

"You've been spurned and I've lost my own naiveté. Neither of us is idealistic any longer. We can help each other."

"We can also hurt each other."

"I'm willing to chance that."

"I'm not," she cried desperately and jumped up from her chair. "You come roaring into my life like a steamroller from out of the past and expect me to fall all over myself. Okay, Mr. Chapman, if it elevates your ego to know, I *did* have a crush on you. I worshiped the ground you walked on. My world revolved around the afternoons I spent with you. Everything I said and did was weighed against what you'd think of it. When my boyfriend kissed me, I pretended it was you. There, does that make you happy? Is that what you wanted to hear?"

"Shelley—"

"But I'm not a starry-eyed teenager anymore. If you're looking for that kind of blind devotion, look someplace else."

He closed the distance between them in several long strides. With angry hands he took her shoulders and shook her slightly. "Is that what you think I want from you? Hero worship? Infatuation? No, Shelley. You're an intelligent woman and I respect your intelligence. But I want you as a lover, too. Naked and passionate and as hot for me as I am for you. And don't try telling me that the thought of us together like that has never crossed your mind. You've all but admitted as much."

He shook her again. "Didn't you ever wonder what would have happened had I obeyed my impulse that night, carried you out of there, undressed you, looked at you, touched you, caressed you? By God I did, and cursed the morality that prevented me from ever seeing your body and touching it and tasting it and making love to it."

She groaned and tried to bury her face in his

shirtfront, but he wouldn't let her. He captured her face between his hands and tilted it up to his. "You didn't have a happy love life with your husband. You didn't like making love to him, did you, Shelley?"

"Please," she moaned and tried to escape his hands. He wouldn't allow it.

"You didn't like it, did you?" he demanded.

She held her breath for a moment, then shook her head furiously. "No," she whispered, then said more forcefully, "no, no, no."

"Ah, God." He crushed her to him, rocking her back and forth slowly. His fingers laced through her hair to fit over her scalp and pressed her face against his chest. His lips brushed over her hair in a fervent kiss. After a while, he lifted her chin with his thumb.

His finger followed the heart shape of her hairline. "You're so beautiful." He mouthed the words rather than said them, but she understood. "I love the smoky color of your eyes, the shape of your mouth." He outlined it with his fingertip. "Your hair is soft and shiny and natural, not twisted into some contrived shape." He leaned down and pressed his lips against hers. "You need to be loved, Shelley, by someone who appreciates the woman you are. Let me love you."

"I don't know, Grant."

"We're on your timetable. No pressure." He kissed her then. His kiss was a deep and thorough melding of their mouths. He adjusted his body to hers and felt only a tremor of alarm when he cradled his manhood against her. His thumb stroked the warm skin of her neck and pressed against the pulsating vein.

"Will you go to the football game with me Saturday?" The question was a caress against her parted lips. He kissed her again with a gentle love bite on her lower lip. "After the game, the faculty is invited to the chancellor's house for cocktails. Surely you wouldn't be so cruel as to make me suffer through that alone."

She thought his fingertip was gliding along the side of her breast under her arm, but his touch was so tender she couldn't be sure. However, it was enough to make her breathless when she answered, "I guess I'd never forgive myself if I did."

He sampled her mouth one more time, using his tongue like an instrument designed solely to give sensual pleasure. "I'll be by Saturday at two." He kissed her swiftly and hard, then left, closing the door behind him.

"Grant, slow down. Who do you think you are? The star halfback?" Her hand was locked tightly in his as he led her through the maze of the stadium parking lot toward the gates swarming with football enthusiasts.

"Sorry," he said, slowing down. "I didn't think an ol' cheerleader like you would want to miss the kickoff."

Ever since she had accepted his invitation, she had anguished over consenting to this date. Common sense dictated that she should have told him no. But each time she was with him, common sense seemed to desert her. If he felt confident enough to take her to the home of the chancellor of the university, why should she feel timorous about it?

She had answered his knock with a high sense of anticipation, and it was rewarded. He looked gorgeous. His dark hair was mussed as usual, but it gleamed in the autumn sunshine. He was dressed in a sport shirt and slacks that perfectly accentuated the lean, tough virility of his physique.

"You look great," he said, taking in her striped skirt and a silk shirt that matched the cloudy-sky color of her eyes. Without pause or awkwardness, he drew her into his embrace and kissed her with the hunger of a starved man. After the initial shock of his thrusting intimacy had subsided, she wound her arms around his neck.

When at last they parted, each with a thudding heart and shortness of breath, he brought his lips against her ear and said, "We could skip the football game and have our own little match right here. I'll referee and keep score. All you have to do is play along."

She blushed furiously and shoved him aside to gather her blue wool blazer and suede purse. He was still laughing when he settled her into his sleek black Datsun 280 Z. They joked and teased while he negotiated his way through the heavy traffic on the way to the stadium. For the first time, they were relaxed with each other, meeting on equal ground as two adults, forgetting the dismal past and enjoying only the present.

"Aren't football games fun?" he was growling in her ear now. They had been consumed by the throng. To keep them from getting separated, he had wrapped his arms around her waist and positioned her in front of him. He held her tight against him as they made their way slowly toward the ramp that led to their reserved seats.

His meaning didn't escape her. She could feel the straining pressure of his masculinity against her hips. His breath in her ear, against her cheek, on the back of her neck, was a sweet airy caress. "I think you're taking unfair advantage."

"And you're absolutely right." He moved his arm up a fraction until it lay just below her breasts. No one in the mob would have noticed. "But can you blame a guy when he's with the most beautiful woman on the whole campus?"

"Even more beautiful than Miss Zimmerman?" Shelley said with unusual cattiness, referring to the girl who had spoken to him outside Hal's. "She's obviously attracted to you and she certainly has a *couple* of fine attributes."

"I like your attributes better."

He jostled his arm enough to lift her breasts slightly and to convey his message loud and clear. Shelley's sharp gasp caused the man beside her to whip his head around.

"Pardon me. Did I step on your foot?"

She shook her head. "No." Grant's chest vibrated with silent laughter.

They located their seats in time for the kickoff and were soon caught up in the excitement of the season opener. The afternoon was glorious. The sun was shining, though a northern breeze kept the temperature moderate. By the end of the third quarter Shelley had grown warm beneath her blazer and asked Grant to help her out of it.

After that she felt much more comfortable, but couldn't help noticing Grant's increasing restlessness. He wasn't able to sit still even during lulls in the game.

"Is something wrong?" she asked, concerned. He didn't look unwell. On the contrary, he looked spectacular to her, the epitome of manhood. He had a wildness, a recklessness, about him that caused an aftershock in the system of every woman who came in contact with him. "Is something wrong?" she repeated, when he seemed disinclined to answer her.

"No," he said brusquely. "Far from it." He muttered a curse under his breath.

The home team executed an intricate play to gain twenty-five yards and the crowd rose to its feet, cheering with frenzy. Heedless, Shelley placed an anxious hand on Grant's arm. "Grant?" she inquired worriedly.

He fixed her with the eyes that had been the subject of so many of her fantasies and asked, "Did you have to wear such a revealing blouse?"

Dumbstruck she looked down at her chest. The blouse itself was not particularly revealing, but the wind, deceptively mild, had molded the silk to the voluptuous curves beneath it, detailing her form. Unable to meet his eyes, she struggled to pull on her blazer again and then feigned absorption in the activities on the field.

The game progressed to a climactic conclusion,

the home team scoring a touchdown in the final two minutes. Exiting the stadium was just as slow as entering had been. They walked side by side, his hand closed around the back of her neck, their hips bumping together as they walked.

"I wasn't complaining, you know," he said, causing her to blush.

"It wasn't intentional," she said tartly, pausing to face him until the tide of spectators shoved them forward again.

"I never thought it was. I'm sorry if what I said embarrassed you."

The sincerity in his voice and eyes was too real to discount. She smiled her forgiveness. "And I'm sorry I acted so defensively."

He squeezed the back of her neck lightly in understanding.

Once in his car and waiting in the line of traffic to leave the parking lot he said, "Do you mind stopping by my apartment? I have to change shirts and pick up a tie."

"Fine," she said, smiling, though her heart lurched at the thought of being alone with him again without the protection of a crowd of witnesses.

His duplex was a few blocks off campus in one of the more modern sections of town, an area no less quiet and private than Shelley's neighborhood. He opened her door and helped her out of the low-slung car, escorting her up the stone walkway to his front door, which was flush with the straight Georgian facade of the house.

"I don't have a cozy front porch like yours," he said.

"But you have a wonderful apartment," she replied, stepping inside. The lower level consisted of one large room with a fireplace and big paned windows. Behind louvered barroom doors, she could see a tiny kitchen. A spiral staircase led to a bedroom loft. One circular table in the main room was littered with textbooks on government and law, the thickness of which intimidated her. Magazines and records were piled onto bookshelves. Folders were stuffed into filing cabinets. It was neat, but well lived in.

"There's a half bath on the other side of the kitchen if you need to freshen up," he said, winding his way up the staircase.

"I'm fine. I think I'll repair my makeup though." She riffled through her purse, wishing her fingers would not shake so. She finally gave up finding a lipstick and opened her mirror compact.

It nearly went flying from her hand when he asked from above her. "How're you doing down there? You're as quiet as a mouse."

"Fine, I—" Whatever she had been about to say never made it past the congestion in her throat. He was splashing cologne on his cheeks as he leaned over the railing of the loft . . . bare-chested.

His torso was covered with that fine dark hair that seemed to invite a woman to touch it, to test its crinkling texture with her fingertips. She found herself studying the hair just above his gold belt buckle. Vividly she remembered the way it had felt under her hand when she caressed him in the library. Her whole body felt oddly weak, but she couldn't tear her eyes away.

"I'll be right with you," he said, smiling down at her and retreating beyond her range of vision.

Using inordinate care to keep from dropping it, she closed the compact and replaced it in her purse, searching now for her hairbrush. Maybe if she concentrated on such ordinary tasks, she wouldn't think about how he looked or the blood pumping through her veins like rich syrup.

"Dammit."

The muffled curse came from the loft. She heard shuffling movements, another curse. "What is it?"

"A button just came off my shirt and I don't have another clean one that goes with the coat I was going to wear."

"Do you have a sewing kit?"

"Sure."

"Bring it here. I'll see what I can do."

Within seconds, he was loping down the staircase with a speed that would have made her dizzy. "We're in luck. There's some blue thread in here," he said, extracting from the sewing kit a card with several colors of thread wound around it. A slender sewing needle was secured in the cardboard.

She took the sewing implements from him, thankful for something to do so she wouldn't have to look at him. He had left the shirt unbuttoned, and a close-up view of that wonderfully masculine chest was more disturbing than a distant one. "Where's the button?"

"Here." He passed the small white button to her.

"Are you going to . . . to . . . uh, take it off?"

"Can't you sew on the button this way?"

She swallowed. "Sure," she said with a cocky assurance she was far from feeling. Somehow, despite palsied fingers, she managed to thread the needle with the pale blue thread.

"Should we sit down?" he asked.

"No. This is fine."

The button was the third one down from the collar, which placed it in the middle of his chest. Pushing aside a wave of self-consciousness, she took the fine material between her fingers, held it taut and, slipping her other hand under it, pulled the needle through.

She worked as quickly as she could without snarling the thread. Ever aware of his chest just beneath her fingers, she tried to avoid touching him. Invariably, however, she was tickled by springy hairs or warmed by the skin under her hand. There were moments when he didn't seem to be breathing. When his breath was released, she felt it on her forehead and cheeks. She could swear that the dull thudding she heard was his heartbeat, but it might have been her own. By the time she knotted the thread, her senses were reeling.

"Scissors?" she asked huskily.

5

"Scissors?" He repeated the word as though he'd never heard it before. His eyes were staring into hers, peeling away layer after layer of defense until he reached her soul. "I don't know where they are," he said at last.

"Never mind." Not thinking, only wishing to end this project that had completely unnerved her, she leaned forward and caught the thread between her teeth, biting it in two. Not until then did she realize that her lips hovered a fraction of an inch from his chest. Her breath stirred the hair covering it.

"Shelley." He sighed.

His hands came up to touch her hair reverently. She couldn't turn away. Her brain was telling her to step back, escape, flee, but her body refused to obey. Instead she surrendered to the seduction of the moment. She didn't even try to fight the compulsion that swept her toward him with the irrevocability of the tide. Sweetly she nuzzled him with her nose.

"Again, Shelley, again. Please."

Apparently he was as transported by what was happening as she. His voice was uneven and thin, lacking its usual resonance. He placed his thumbs in front of her ears and encircled the back of her head with his strong, slender fingers.

She closed her eyes. When first her lips touched him, they were hesitant. But the graphic reaction of his body encouraged her. She kissed him again, slowly, with measured kisses that charted a path across the expanse of his chest.

When her lips encountered his nipple, she raised her head slightly. She could feel his eyes boring into the top of her head. Seconds stretched out into a small eternity. The hypnotic movement of his hands on her scalp stilled. He waited.

"Should I?" she whispered. "Do you want me to?"

"Do *you* want to?"

She made the decision subconsciously. Before she realized the full implications of the action, her tongue had slipped past her lips to flick over his nipple. Then she teased it further with delicate licks.

Grant gave a short cry before he took her in his arms. "Oh God, you're sweet. So sweet." She tilted her head up and he lowered his mouth to hers. Ravenous lips fused together. His tongue plunged into her mouth and deflowered it, making it his. Careful of the needle she still held in her hand, she hooked her arm around his neck, drawing him downward, closer still. Her other hand splayed on the majestic chest, combed through the forest of hair, pressed the hard muscles.

Her breasts seemed to swell with emotion. He moved away enough to lower his hand and touch them. His knuckles moved gently over the sensitive buds, making them firmer beneath the silk. He fondled her so exquisitely that she called his name against his lips.

"Shelley, did you ever fantasize about this? About my touching you this way?"

"Yes, yes."

"So did I. May God forgive me, but I did, and when you were much too young to figure in this kind of fantasy." His lips moved back and forth across hers. "We can make all our fantasies come true," he urged.

She leaned against him weakly, wanting to give in yet knowing it wouldn't be wise. She loved him. At some point in the last ten years she had come to that indisputable conclusion. He was no longer an idol, the subject of youthful imaginings. He was the man intended for her to love, and she wanted that love to be fulfilled.

But to him, she might only be a novelty. While she had lived an unhappy life, pining for him, thinking of him constantly, dreaming impossible dreams, manufacturing romantic situations in her mind that would never happen, he had been living a hectic, whirlwind life in Washington. Had he really thought of her then, or were his methods of getting her into bed just more sophisticated than Daryl's had been?

She had constructed a new life for herself out of the rubble of her shattered marriage. Her plans for the future were carefully laid out and going according to schedule. Should she let Grant Chapman into her life, he might upset that schedule, if not destroy her plans for the future altogether.

The pain of leaving his embrace was worse than having a dagger pierce her heart, but she gradually pushed against him until he relented and let her go. She turned and walked to the window, staring out at the twilit evening. She heard the rasp of his zipper as he lowered it to tuck his shirttail into his trousers before doing it up again. Her ears picked up the sound of his muted footsteps on the thick rug as he came to stand behind her.

"I was never Missy Lancaster's lover." He hadn't touched her, yet his words caused her to spin around, her eyes wide.

"Grant," she said dolefully, "that has nothing to do with us. I'm reluctant for us to . . . to . . . sleep together, but not because of what happened between you and that girl in Washington."

The relaxing of the lines on either side of his mouth testified to his relief. But his eyes lost none of their intensity. "I'm glad, because there was nothing between Missy and me. At least not what everyone thought. To have told the unmitigated truth would have been to divulge a confidence I couldn't break." His hand came up to grip her shoulders. "Trust me, Shelley. I'm not lying about this."

Her eyes roved his face. There was no disguising the anxiety there. "I believe you, Grant."

He sighed and released his death grip on her shoulders. "Thank you for that." He kissed her lightly on the lips. "Shall we go? I can't jeopardize my position on this faculty by being late to the chancellor's party."

A short time later, they left the duplex. He had retrieved his sportcoat from upstairs and knotted a necktie under his shirt collar. Shelley had retreated to the half bath to freshen her makeup—which truly needed it now—and to brush her hair.

The chancellor lived on an estate owned by the university. Set on a hill, the house was an imposing colonial with six white columns across a broad front porch. Grant parked the Datsun at the foot of the hill and they started up the incline on foot.

His voice was deceptively innocent as he asked, "If the business in Washington wasn't the reason, why did you stop me, Shelley?"

Her footsteps faltered on the gravel driveway. He clasped her elbow and urged her on. "I need more time," she said in a low voice. "I need to know if what I'm feeling now is real or just an extension of what I felt for you ten years ago."

That was a lie. She knew she loved him, always had, always would. But she didn't want him to know that yet. "I'm not sure I want to get involved with anyone right now. I've had a difficult time getting my life together. Now that it looks like I might make something of it, I'm afraid to gamble."

She stopped and faced him. "I haven't changed much since high school. At least where morals are concerned. Sex isn't a casual pastime to me. I couldn't sleep with you one night, and the next day go blithely on my way as though nothing had happened."

His eyes were lit with an internal flame that burned into hers. "I'm glad you feel that way. Because once I slept with you, I doubt I'd ever be able to let you go."

Flabbergasted by what he'd said and the profound way he'd said it, she remained mesmerized by his eyes. Finally, forcing herself out of the trance, she said, "Besides we're still teacher and student."

He tossed his head back and let out a short laugh. "You can always fall back on that, can't you?" She returned his grin as he steered her up the steps to the porch. "Come up with a better excuse, Shelley. Who the hell cares about *that?*"

Chancellor Martin did.

The cocktail—or rather wine—party was as stuffy and dull as Grant had predicted it would be. They were ceremoniously greeted by a receiving line as soon as the butler let them in the door. Chancellor Martin's physical appearance was perfectly suited to his career as an academician. He was austere, gray-haired, high of brow, tall in stature. He handled his introduction to Shelley graciously enough, but she felt that his shrewd blue eyes were sizing her up.

His wife, a stout matron with gray hair a shade bluer than her husband's, spoke to Grant and Shelley with an insincere smile carved onto her face. She seemed more interested in adjusting the cluster of diamonds pinned to her ample bosom than in them.

"Can you imagine Mrs. Martin writhing in the throes of passion?" Grant asked out of the corner of his mouth as they moved away. Shelley nearly dropped her glass of wine. She had accepted it from the silver tray another rented-for-the-evening butler was passing around. She was convulsed with silent laughter.

"Shut up," Shelley ground out between her teeth as she tried to maintain a decorous mien. "You're going to make me spill my wine and then I'll have to have this blouse dry-cleaned, when otherwise I might get by with wearing it one more time."

They mingled, and Shelley couldn't help noticing that the women in the room, faculty members and spouses alike, gravitated to Grant like homing pigeons. She was sickened by their subtle questions, purposely drafted to lead him into a discussion of Missy Lancaster and her suicide. Deftly he managed to detour them to other topics.

The men in the room discussed the afternoon's football game, the season in general and the team's chances for a bowl game. Grant introduced Shelley without explaining who she was, but one of her former professors remembered her just the same. Shelley was sure that news of their student-teacher relationship was spreading through the room.

A half hour later Shelley and Grant found themselves in Chancellor Martin's den. They were discussing the merits of backgammon over chess when the chancellor himself walked in.

"Ah, there you are, Mr. Chapman. I was hoping for a word with you." He sounded friendly enough, but the way he closed the double doors to the room behind him filled Shelley with foreboding.

"We were just admiring this room," Grant said congenially. "It's beautiful, as is the rest of the house."

"Yes, well," he said, coughing unnecessarily, "as you know the university owns the house, but when I was appointed chancellor and we moved in, Marjorie redecorated it."

Moving to the bookcase-lined wall, he clasped his hands behind him and rocked back on his heels. "Mr. Chapman—"

"Excuse me," Shelley said, edging her way toward the door.

"No, Mrs. Robins, as this concerns you, I'll ask you to stay."

She cast a furtive glance in Grant's direction, then said, "All right."

"Now," the chancellor said ponderously, "as you know, this university maintains high standards both academically and morally. We, meaning the board of directors, care about the reputation of this school, both as an institute of higher learning and as a community unto itself. Because we are a church-sponsored university, we must safeguard that reputation. Therefore," he said, swiveling his head around and glaring at them in a gesture guaranteed to strike terror into the heart of any miscreant, "the members of the faculty must have sterling reputations on campus and off."

A deathly quiet had descended over the room.

Neither Grant nor Shelley spoke or moved, but out of the corner of her eye she saw that Grant's fists were clenched at his sides.

"We took a chance in hiring you to teach at this university, Mr. Chapman. The board reviewed your application carefully. They felt that you were unfairly exploited by the press in Washington. They benevolently gave you the benefit of the doubt.

"Your credentials are excellent. When you publish, as you've expressed a desire to do, that will lend further distinction to the university. But your keeping company with a student, albeit an older one, leaves you vulnerable to criticism and puts the university in an unfavorable light. Especially after the unfortunate affair so recently publicized. I must request that you and Mrs. Robins, whose status as a divorcée only adds another questionable element to the situation, stop seeing each other on a social basis."

Grant wasn't impressed by either the chancellor's edict or his piety. "Or else what?" he asked calmly. The controlled tone wasn't in keeping with the fierce expression on his face.

"Or else we might have to review your contract at the end of the semester," Chancellor Martin said.

Grant crossed to Shelley and took her arm. "You have not only insulted me and questioned my morality, which I'm sure is in keeping with that of the university, but you have maligned Mrs. Robins—"

"Grant—"

"—whose reputation is spotless."

She had tried to interrupt, afraid that he'd say

something in her defense that would further antagonize the chancellor. For judging by the pallor of his face, few, if any, had ever ignored his warnings.

"Thank you for your hospitality," Grant was saying as he dragged her toward the door. "And thank Mrs. Martin for us."

He flung the door open wide, strode through it proudly and wended his way through those lingering at the party to the front door. If he noticed heads curiously turning in his wake, he didn't show it. Shelley only prayed that the color in her cheeks wasn't as vivid as she felt it was and that her knees would continue to support her until they were at least through the front door.

In fact, they held up until she reached the car. As soon as Grant opened the door of the passenger side she slumped into the seat, overcome by trembling.

It wasn't until Grant had sped down the lane to the main thoroughfare and wheeled the sports car into the sparse traffic that he said, "I'm starving. What sounds good to you? Pizza?"

She turned her head to stare at him with incredulity. "Pizza! Grant, the chancellor of the university just threatened to fire you."

"Something he can't do without a majority vote from the board. And despite the adverse publicity I've received and the aura of scandal that surrounds me, some of them are star-struck and want to keep me around. Others realize that I'm a damn good teacher.

"The only thing that makes me mad as hell is what he said about you. That sanctimonious jackass. If he had the opportunity, don't think he wouldn't like to see you on a 'social basis.'"

"Grant!" Shelley cried before covering her face with her hands. Her obvious distress sobered him. After covering the distance to her house in silence, save for an occasional muffled sob from Shelley, he whipped the car to the curb and braked abruptly. His earlier suggestion about dinner was forgotten.

For long moments they sat in stony silence. Grant's profile, lit by the soft glow of the streetlight outside the car's window, was just as forbidding as that of Chancellor Martin. Shelley gathered enough courage to say, "We can't see each other anymore, Grant. Not like today."

He turned in the bucket seat to face her, his clothes making a rustling sound in the darkness. He braced his arm on the back of his seat and gave her a level stare. "You're really going to let a parody of respectability like Martin keep us apart?"

She exhaled wearily. "I know what he is, and if he didn't hold the position he does, I wouldn't give him or his opinion a thought. But he *is* the chancellor of the university and you *are* in his employ."

"There was no clause in my contract about whom I date."

"But it's an unwritten law that teachers don't date their students. I tried to tell you weeks ago what people around here would think of us. You wouldn't listen. This isn't the more progressive-thinking East or West Coast. This is mid-America. Such things just aren't done."

"What are we doing that's so bad?" he shouted, finally losing the composure he'd tried so hard to hold on to. When he saw her flinch, he cursed under his breath and let out a long, exasperated sigh. "I'm sorry. I'm not angry at you."

"I know," she said quietly. It was the hopelessness of the situation that angered him.

Grant found it hard to admit to that, however. "I don't want another upheaval in my life. Hell, that's the last thing I want. I especially don't want one that could in any way touch you. But dammit, I can't give you up either."

"You'll have to. How do you think I'd feel if you lost your job on account of me? Do you think I could live with that?"

"I've lived through much worse, Shelley. Believe me, I'm a survivor. It wouldn't bother me."

"Well, it would bother me a great deal." She placed her hand on the door handle. "Good-bye, Grant."

He caught her arm with a hand like a steel talon. "I won't let them force us apart no matter what they threaten. And I won't let you throw it all away. Shelley, I need you. I want you. And I know you want me just as much."

His other hand shot across the interior of the car and caught the back of her neck, hauling her against him. "No—" she managed to force out before he clamped his mouth over hers. The kiss was brutal, his passion adding to his frustration.

Holding her motionless with one hand, he slid the other down to trap her breast. His rotating palm coaxed the nipple into rapid response. Then fingers talented in the art of seduction finessed it into rigid proof of her building desire.

"Please no," she breathed into his mouth as his kiss gentled, "don't touch me anymore." His tongue glided along her lower lip, sliding over it to caress the soft interior just beyond.

"Don't deny us this, Shelley. After all this time, don't take this away from us. Haven't we paid enough dues for the privilege? I want to know all of you."

He began with her ear. It was explored thoroughly by a velvet-rough tongue that whimsically probed or teased. Her hand had unconsciously closed over his thigh. She squeezed the muscled flesh beneath his trousers mindlessly, gripping it harder when his touch raised the level of her excitement.

Had Grant not already been driven with his need to possess her, the placement of her hand would have provided him with more than enough incentive. As it was, her unconscious caress only fanned the fires of his passion and made him more determined than ever to eliminate her fears and reluctance.

His mouth sampled the smooth skin of her neck and chest, alternately nibbling with his teeth and stroking with his tongue. She felt herself welcoming the rising storm inside her. She wanted to be drawn into the tempest, into the maelstrom his caresses made of her universe.

Impatient with her clothes, he kissed her through them. He pressed hot, moist kisses onto the lush curves of her breasts. When he reached her nipple, she gasped his name and wound his hair around her fingers.

His tongue feathered the agitated peak, burning through the blue silk and the sheer veil of her brassiere. Her breath came in quick, shallow pants as his tongue nudged her breast more insistently, and she cried his name sharply when his mouth closed around the tip completely.

He tugged on her gently. First one breast, then the other received his meticulous attention. He lifted his mouth free only long enough to speak her name in a loving chant.

She welcomed him when his hand insinuated itself under her skirt and slip to stroke her thigh. The silky texture of her panty hose only heightened her sensitivity. She liquified under his touch, moving in a way that encouraged his bold exploration.

Aroused as they were, neither was prepared for the tumult of emotion that rocked them when his caressing hand reached the top of her thighs. He pressed his forehead against her breasts while her fingers remained enmeshed in his dark hair.

He whispered endearments as his thumb erotically stroked the gently swelling mound and her thighs relaxed and parted. "Shelley, I've got to love you," he said as he opened his hand to enclose her.

This was the man she'd always wanted and here he was, offering her unbound passion. Why was she reluctant to accept it? Because this wasn't a fairy tale. This was life. Things like this didn't happen in the real world. No man, whom a woman loved and desired for years, came back into her life like a knight on a white charger. Nothing worked out that perfectly. Somewhere, at some time, a price had to be paid.

It would be so easy to submit to his whispered words of love and her own blazing desire. She wanted him, thought she might very well die if she didn't have him, but she couldn't stake both their careers on one night's pleasure. And that was all it might be.

He was willing to gamble on an affair. After all, he could always walk away from it. When he was through with her, when he had broken her heart all over again, he could simply retreat. He'd be free and she'd be left to pick up the pieces of her life again.

She didn't really think Grant could be so callous. But then she hadn't thought Daryl could be either. When it came right down to it, women were at the mercy of the men they loved.

Much as she loved Grant, she wasn't going to be that vulnerable again.

At first he didn't realize that she was struggling to extricate herself from him, not to move closer. The sudden stiffening of her limbs alerted him as nothing else could. Her hands warded him off. He looked at her blankly, blinked and shook his head to clear it.

"Shelley . . . ?"

"Good-bye, Grant." She shoved open the car door and tumbled out.

"Shelley!" she heard him shout. She ran up the walk, let herself in the house and slammed the front door as though the devil were after her.

Like an automaton that knew exactly how to act but was void of feeling, she went into her bedroom and climbed out of her clothes. She looked down at the two damp stains on the front of her blouse with dismay. It would have to be dry-cleaned after all, she realized as she burst into tears.

She spent Sunday cloistered in her house. Since it rained all day, she had a good excuse to remain indoors. Her mother called and asked if there was anything new in her life and if she was enjoying this semester's classes. Shelley elected not to mention her political-science teacher.

Apparently Grant was going to let her decision stand. She had expected him to telephone, but he didn't.

Monday night she debated with herself about attending Grant's class the next day or dropping it as she had threatened to do a week ago. The reasons for dropping it were obvious. Yet she found herself coming up with reasons for staying in the class.

First, she didn't want to give Chancellor Martin the satisfaction of having cowed her. Not that he would ever know one way or another, but she couldn't tolerate the thought of giving in so easily.

Secondly, she didn't want Grant to think her a coward. He had called her that once and he wasn't far from wrong, but she didn't want him to think her cowardly. She had boasted that she had put her life in order, that she was independent, self-sufficient. If she knuckled under at the first sign of trouble and retreated without dignity, he would think her an utter fool, immature and not worthy of the attention he'd already given her. That stung. She couldn't abide that.

On Tuesday, with eyes red from crying, and grim resolution engraved on her delicate features, she went into the classroom. Grant was standing, bending over his desk perusing his notes. The muscle spasm in his jaw was a dead giveaway that he knew she had come in, but he didn't deign to look up.

That set the pattern for the next two weeks. He never looked at her as if truly seeing her. On several occasions, she was tempted to contribute to the heated discussions he encouraged in the class, but she refrained. She could maintain this vigil of silence as long as he.

One afternoon when she purposely arrived early in an attempt to force Grant to speak to her, she caught him in the company of Miss Zimmerman.

The younger girl was perched on the corner of his desk in a most seductive and not at all subtle way. He was laughing up at her as he sat tilting his chair back on two legs, his feet propped on the corner of the desk close to her hip. Shelley gnashed her teeth in an effort to quell the temptation to kick the legs of his chair out from under him and to slap Miss Zimmerman resoundingly on her overrouged cheek.

Thoroughly enraged with him and disgusted with herself for caring, she didn't take one note during his lecture. The view out the window absorbed her total attention as she sat fuming at her desk. At the conclusion of the class, she yanked up her books and flounced past him on her way to the door.

"Mrs. Robins?"

Her feet came to an abrupt halt, causing the student immediately behind her to bump into her.

She toyed with the idea of ignoring the summons, but the other students had heard Grant address her. Besides, she didn't want to provide him with more fuel to ridicule her. Stiffening her spine and straightening her shoulders, she turned to meet his gray-green eyes.

"Yes?" she said as coldly as she could, though her blood had begun to heat the moment he spoke her name.

"I need a research assistant and grader. Would you be interested in the job . . . Mrs. Robins?"

6

The stream of students leaving the classroom eddied around her as she stood stock-still and stared at him. What did he think she was, a puppet that danced when he pulled the right string? He hadn't spoken to her in weeks and now he was asking her to be his assistant.

"I . . . I don't think so, Mr. Chapman," she said frostily.

Before she turned away, he hurriedly added, "At least let me detail the job for you, then if you're not interested I'll ask someone else."

On the surface their conversation appeared quite ordinary. But the polite words hid suppressed sexual awareness and antagonism. Shelley wanted to lash out at him for ignoring her the last few weeks, and at the same time to fling herself into his arms, begging to be held.

She despised that weakness in herself but was mature and honest enough to admit that it was there. Refusing to betray her emotions, she kept her face impassive, objective. Her posture was militarily straight.

When the last student had left and the door had closed, Grant said calmly, "Sit down, Mrs. Robins."

"I'm in a hurry, Mr. Chapman. I prefer to stand. I'm not interested in becoming your assistant."

He shook his head and ran a hand around the back of his neck in irritation. She was reminded of his description of a professor and wanted to laugh. He looked like anything but that. His slacks were tailored to perfection, fitting his narrow hips like a glove. A dark plaid cotton shirt in muted shades of gray, green and rust stretched over the sleek muscles of his chest and shoulders. She tore her eyes away from the wedge of dark hair in the "V" of his collar and raised her gaze to his.

Meeting his eyes proved to be a reckless mistake. They were looking at her with far too soft an expression. The hunger she read there mirrored her own.

"I need someone to do research for me, Mrs. . . . damn . . . *Shelley.* It would involve extra reading on your part with reports back to me. Oral reports, not written. We have an exam next week and I need help in grading. I have five classes of forty or more students each."

She studied the toe of her boot. It wasn't nearly

as interesting as his male form, but it was safer. When she was looking at him, sound judgment deserted her. She forced a hard finality into her voice. "I can't help you."

He went on as though she hadn't spoken. "You're an excellent student. I know your class schedule is heavy this semester, but I doubt your grade average is less than a two-point-five now. You don't work and have no family obligations. And I need you."

Her eyes flew to his face. Those words were an echo of what she'd heard before. The deprivation on his face made her suspect a double entendre. But his choice of words had served his purpose. She felt the last fine threads of resistance snapping.

"I'm sure you could find someone else," she said a trifle shakily.

"I'm sure I could, too. But I don't want anyone else. I want you."

The stiff posture she had imposed on herself gradually relaxed until her shoulders took on their normal feminine softness. Avoiding his moss-colored eyes, she looked out the window at the gray, blustery day.

"Wh—where would you want to work?"

"The most logical place is my duplex. All the texts are there. They're too heavy for you to carry around. I have an excellent filing system for exams, etcetera."

She was shaking her head. "That would be insane, Grant." Rather than tell him she couldn't bear sharing that cozy room with him, she used an excuse. "If Chancellor Martin ever found out—"

"I'd tell him I needed an assistant, which is the truth, and that you are my best student, which is also the truth."

She faced him with as much composure as she could. "I'm sure it would be preferable if this assistant you need so much were a male student."

For the first time, the corners of his mouth tilted into a ghost of a smile. "Preferable for whom?" He coaxed a shadowy smile from her, too, before he said with soft earnestness, "I've missed you, Shelley."

"Don't," she choked, lowering her eyes again and shaking her head. She cursed the tears she felt pooling in her eyes. "Please, don't. Don't make it harder than it is."

"*You're* making it harder than it is. I told you we were on your timetable, but I can't stand this state of limbo any longer."

"You've ignored me for almost three weeks," she cried with wounded feminine pride. "I might just as well have been dead."

"Oh no, Shelley. I was all too aware of you. Perversely I hoped you were suffering as much as I. Each night I lay in bed thinking of you, your smell, your feel, your taste."

"No . . ."

"I want you so bad I ache." He stepped forward and placed his hands on her shoulders. "Shelley—" The door opened.

"Mr. Chap—Well excuse me," the coed drawled

insinuatingly. Indolently she leaned against the opened door, a sly look narrowing her eyes.

Shelley dashed the tears from her cheeks and turned toward the window. She folded her arms across her waist in a defensive gesture.

"What is it, Miss Zimmerman?" Grant asked tersely.

Not one to be intimidated, the girl met his stern expression with an insolent smile. "Nothing. It can wait. Later," she said and walked out the door, firmly closing it behind her.

For a tension-laden moment neither moved, then Grant came toward her. "Shelley, I'm sor—"

She whirled around to face him. "Why don't you ask her to be your assistant? She seems more than willing to do anything for you."

The surprised look on his face gave her a feeling of satisfaction but didn't begin to abate her anger. Irrationally she was taking out her self-directed fury on him. She was no better than the others throwing themselves at him, craving his touch. How many hearts was he dangling along? That she could be one of a harem enraged her. "I'm sure your Miss Zimmerman or someone like her is just dying to spend long evenings with you poring over your dusty textbooks."

Grant had a hard time keeping his own temper in check. She could tell by the way his jaw was working and the way he held his arms stiffly at his sides. "She's not 'my' Miss Zimmerman. What the hell does she have to do with anything anyway? She's a silly little coed. So? Give me some credit,

Shelley," he said with exasperation. "Now, are you going to help me or not?"

It was a challenge, bold and uncompromising. She had to meet it head-on. "Yes, I'll help you. I'll do your research and I'll grade for you. But this is strictly a business arrangement."

"Very well."

"I mean it. Strictly business."

"I understand."

They were both lying and they both knew it. This face-off had nothing to do with business, but it suited their purpose at the time to pretend that it did.

"What are you going to pay me?"

He muttered a curse beneath his breath and shoved his hands into the pockets of his slacks, pulling the cloth taut over his hips. She averted her eyes. "How does twenty dollars a week sound? Two nights a week."

"I like the sound of forty dollars a week better. Twenty dollars a night, three hours maximum, seven to ten."

"Agreed," he growled. "I'll expect you tonight."

"I have an economics quiz I need to study for tonight. You can expect me tomorrow night."

"Okay," he said tightly. "I'll pick you up."

"I'll drive myself."

Aggravation and frustration formed a tangible aura around him. He was fairly bristling. "You know where I live."

"Yes. See you at seven sharp, Mr. Chapman."

She marched past him, opened the door and

sailed out before she could give in to the impulse to bury her hands in his thick, unruly hair and beg him to kiss her.

"You're right on time," he said, answering her knock on his door the following evening.

"I promised to be."

"Come in." He was wearing a ragged pair of jeans and a sweat shirt with the sleeves cut out. His bare feet had been pushed into docksiders. Seeing him so casually attired made her heart pound and her hands go clammy, but she passed him coolly and entered the apartment.

She was dressed in a starched white shirt with a pleated front and a narrow black string tie. Her skirt was black wool. A prim ponytail contributed to the crisp and efficient look she knew it was essential to create. She regarded the mountains of paper littering his coffee table and floor with assumed distaste.

"Where should I start?"

He hung her cape on a rack near the door and indicated with a sweep of his hand that she should precede him into the room. "I'd like you to go through these three books—I'll tell you the chapters—and cite instances when the Congress has overridden a presidential veto. Also note if the bill passed was eventually beneficial and list the reasons why. It'll make a good exam question and if a student has read the material, he should be able to give several good examples."

"Won't I be taking the same exam?"

"You'll get alternate questions."

She nodded, not thinking about what was being

said, not thinking of anything except how marvelous his eyes were.

He looked at her for a long while, tension emanating from him. His eyes drifted down to her mouth, but lingered only an instant before he said gruffly, "I'll be working over here if you have any questions."

For the rest of the evening they shared the room, but nothing else. He treated her with professional detachment. As she adjusted herself into a comfortable position on the sofa he turned on the stereo system, then went to the heaped table and began wading through his own stack of books.

After an hour or more he got up and stretched, raising his arms high over his head. Shelley happened to glance up and catch a glimpse of the skin between the hem of his sweat shirt and his low-riding jeans. His navel, thatched with the dark silky hair her fingers remembered, took on a forbidden, erotic aspect when seen accidentally this way. The flagrant manner in which his threadbare jeans detailed his manhood made her heart thud painfully against her ribs.

Licking suddenly dry lips, she dragged her eyes back down to the page she was studying, though for the next few minutes the blurred words wouldn't come into focus.

"Coke?" he called to her over the barroom doors.

"Yes. Please." He came back into the room carrying two tall, iced glasses. He set one on a coaster on the coffee table. "Thank you," she said crisply.

"You're welcome," he replied politely.

At precisely ten o'clock she put her pen in her purse, neatly stacked the pages on which she'd written the required information and stood up. She carried the papers to the table.

"All done, Shelley?" His eyes were watching the rapid rise and fall of her breasts.

"Yes, I've finished, but if my notes need clarification, I'll be glad to explain them." His bare arms looked beautiful in the soft lighting. The curvature of the smooth muscles was accented by light and shadow. She wanted to touch him, to lovingly caress him, much as a sculptor would admire the handiwork he had created out of clay.

"I'm sure they're clear and concise." He stood. "Do I pay you in cash?"

He was much too close and she retreated to the door. She avoided looking at him, pulling on her cape instead. "No. You can give me a check every two weeks or so."

"Fine."

The low huskiness of his voice just behind her was an attraction not to be resisted. Her chin grazed her shoulder as she looked up at him. "Good night." Her hand was on the doorknob, but she hesitated in turning it. She wished he'd say something, do something, demand that they end this ridiculous farce. At that moment, when her body was screaming for her to relent, she would gladly have obeyed him and thrown away the last vestiges of circumspection. Why didn't he reach for her, caress her, kiss her?

His expression was wooden, expressing nothing

of the raging war inside him. His farewell was short and clipped. "Good night."

At the next evening session, she graded exams. He'd given her a list of points each essay should cover. "Just mark them. I'll put the grade on later."

In the same awkward manner as before, they settled down to work. The silence wasn't interrupted until the telephone rang. Grant hauled himself up from the sofa, where he'd been stretched out on his back, the exam book he was reading propped on his chest.

"Hello," he said into the receiver when he picked up the telephone on the end table. "No, Miss Zimmerman, I don't think it's been graded yet. . . . No, you'll find out your grade when everyone else does. . . . Well, I can appreciate that, but . . . No. Good-bye." He hung up with a sigh of irritation. "That girl never gives up!"

"Pru?"

He turned to Shelley with a disbelieving scowl wrinkling his brow. "Pru?"

She held up the coed's exam, which she had graded minutes earlier. "Short for Prudence. It's written right here. P-R-U-D-E-N-C-E with quotation marks around the first three letters."

He threw back his head and roared with laughter. "Boy, if that's not a misnomer I don't know what is."

"Does she call often?" Shelley asked casually as she neatly stacked the exam books she'd already read.

"Jealous?"

"No," she said shortly, but the smoky hue in her blue eyes told him of the fire smoldering just beneath the surface.

He grinned wickedly. "She calls on the days she doesn't leave something in the classroom that she has to come back for or when she doesn't accidentally run into me in the Student Center. She's about as subtle as a locomotive."

Shelley was about to tell him she didn't think one of his female students should be calling him, but what gave her the right? When it came right down to it, she and Pru Zimmerman were on an equal footing. "She's attractive in a blowsy sort of way," she said offhandedly.

"Is 'blowsy' another way of saying she's got big bosoms?"

Her mouth dropped open in stunned surprise and he laughed at her expression. Miffed, she snapped her mouth shut again. "I see you noticed," she said through stiff lips.

He laughed harder. "I'd notice a bulldozer if it were coming at me all the time, too."

"You poor thing," she said. "You can't help it if every girl on campus is smitten, can you?"

His smile suddenly changed into a fierce frown. "You're a fine one to talk. I've seen that guy who sits next to you making cow eyes across the aisle." His expression softened somewhat. "I guess I ought to thank you for keeping him awake during class." He walked toward her until he was only inches away. She had to tilt her head back to look into his face. "I can empathize. Fantasies about you have been keeping me awake, too."

Her mouth went dry and she looked away as she stood up quickly. "It's time for me to go," she said hoarsely, stepping around him and bruising her hip against the table in her haste to leave.

Surprisingly he didn't try to stop her, but he tracked her like a hunter as she went around the room picking up her purse, her coat, a folder she'd brought along.

"Shelley?"

"Yes?" she said, whirling around to face him before her name had completely left his lips.

His eyes roamed her face, lingering a long time on her mouth. "Nothing," he said with a sigh. "Is it all right if we work Friday night? I have a department meeting Thursday evening."

"Yes."

"See you then."

"Is that rain?"

Grant rose from his deep chair and crossed to the window, sliding open one panel of louvers. "Yes. It's raining hard."

"It was cold when I came in this evening."

She had almost been late. That afternoon her honors sorority had hosted a tea for the women on the faculty. She'd stayed afterward to help with the cleanup and, since she was running late, had walked to Grant's duplex. It was closer than the lot where she had parked her car earlier in the day.

She had arrived out of breath, still wearing her gray georgette blouse under a tailored slate-blue suit. "Did someone just get married?" he had quipped when he answered her knock. He was wearing the jeans that seemed to be his uniform while at home and a gold crew-neck sweater.

They had worked silently for hours. Now, with the stack of exams they were grading almost done, Shelley had raised her head when she heard the patter of rain on the roof two stories overhead.

"Would you like a fire? You've had your feet curled up under you for the past hour and I know how cold they can get."

His words were a poignant reminder of the night in the library when his own hands had warmed her feet. Their eyes held for an instant before she looked at the fireplace wistfully. "You shouldn't bother. There are only a few exams left to grade and then it'll be time for me to go."

"No bother," he said, kneeling down to the grate to arrange the firewood and kindling that had previously been stored on the hearth.

While he coaxed the wood into flame, Shelley read through two more exams, making notations in the margins. She was concentrating on an indecipherable essay when the overhead light suddenly went out, plunging the room into darkness, save for the light from the fireplace.

She raised her head and saw Grant just lowering his hand from the light switch on the wall. In the flickering light he appeared larger, stronger, more masculine than ever. The firelight touched the planes of his face and cast the hollows into deep shadow. The stark contrast made his expression impossible to read, but the predatory gait with which he walked toward her announced his intent.

She unfolded her legs and put her stockinged feet on the floor as though preparing to run. "I've got one more exam to grade," she said tremulously.

"It can wait. I can't. I've already waited ten years."

He stood in front of the deep easy chair which had been her station all night. The reflection of the flames danced in the depths of his eyes as she lifted her head to look at him. He brought his hand up to brush a vagrant strand of dark hair from her brow. His fingers cupped her jaw; his thumb stroked her cheek, which was unusually warm and rosy.

Her eyes closed when his thumb brushed over her mouth. Her lips parted under his gentle persuasion and the pad of his thumb ventured between her teeth to touch her tongue. Wet with the nectar of her own mouth, his thumb bathed her bottom lip.

Her breath caught in her lungs when his hands moved down her throat to rest against its base. He pressed each fingertip into the hollow triangle there while his thumb paid homage to the delicacy of her collarbone.

A delicious lethargy seemed to seep into her body through his fingers and she luxuriated in it. How could she be held responsible for what might happen when his touch rendered her helpless?

But the languor was dispelled when his index finger began to trace the collar of her blouse to its deep "V." She opened her eyes wide to meet his. One look into his face and all caution, restraint and inhibition were forgotten.

His face was a study of desire. His eyes glowed with passion. Through his lips, his uneven breath whispered like a love tribute to the woman his hands were honoring. One was gently supporting the back of her head as she gazed up at him, while the other was marveling over the silkiness of her skin.

Her heart stopped beating only to begin racing when his hand paused at the first button on her blouse. He waited, savoring the moment, the firelight, the rain, the transported look on her face. Then his fingers released the fabric-covered button from its loop. He pressed her heart, as if to catch each throbbing beat in his palm.

The second button fell away under his deft manipulation, yet neither of them moved. Each was transfixed as they continued to stare at each other.

At first it was only the tip of his index finger that glided along the lace border of her gray satin slip. Then three others joined it, charting the swell of her breasts beneath the lace. His harsh breathing matched her own. She smiled tentatively, and he returned the smile, but it relieved none of the intensity on his face.

He feathered the side of her breast with trailing fingers that curved to the underside. He tested her fullness in the palm of his hand. Even though his other hand still held it, her head fell back and her throat arched. A low moan of pleading escaped her lips. He kept her waiting no longer.

He maneuvered the satin strap of her slip down into her sleeve far enough so that he could pull away the lacy fabric covering her. For a long while he looked at her—ivory infused with a glowing life of its own. His soft exclamation of delight brought her eyes open again.

With infinite care he touched her, marveling over the round plumpness that was deceptively small beneath her clothes, but which filled his hand. He circled the swollen nipple, then aroused her still further by tenderly rolling it between his fingers. A sound that was half sigh, half sob came out of her throat and she leaned forward. Frantically she groped for a handhold to keep her on the world, to keep her from flying out into space.

Her hand buried itself under his sweater and four fingers dug past the waistband of his jeans, gripping the denim between them and her thumb on the outside. She rested her forehead against his stomach and moved it back and forth as he performed his sweet torment on her breast. His hand, cupped behind her head, pressed her closer.

"Grant, Grant," she repeated in a sexual cadence matching the tempo of his caressing fingertips. Her slip had worked down beneath her breasts. His hand roamed seemingly without direction, yet touched her in such a way that wave after wave of pleasure washed over her. "Please . . ." she panted. Her hand tugged, trying to pull him down.

Finally he knelt beside her. He held her face between his palms and drew it close to his. "Shelley, I love you." His sweet, hot breath struck her lips. "There'll be no stopping me."

She shook her head. "I don't want you to stop."

With hands sure and eager, she clasped his head and drew him down to her breast. He kissed the lush, fragrant flesh with abandon, dropping ardent, damp kisses at random. When his mouth fastened on her nipple and suckled gently, she arched her back instinctively. His hand slid around her, found the groove of her spine and urged her upward and forward.

When his primary, savage hunger had been satisfied, he finessed her more tenderly, plucking at her softly with his lips, then laving her with his tongue. Her hands gloried in his thick dark hair, weaving it between her fingers. She stroked his temples and cheekbones with her thumbs.

He kissed his way up to her mouth and made love to it. Tongues battled, conquered, submitted.

"May I undress you?" he asked against the velvet spot beneath her ear.

"Yes."

He pulled the tangled blouse from her shoulders and brought the slip to her waist. Slowly he stood and raised her with him. He unbuttoned her skirt, undid the zipper, and both skirt and slip drifted to the floor. He helped her to step free of them. His eyes traveled down her torso and his hands followed their lead.

He closed them over her breasts, not with passion, but with reverence, and kissed her sweetly on the mouth before he lowered himself to his knees again. Her panty hose were tinted gray and had a sheer lacy panty. He kissed her through the lace.

When he lowered the garment, he placed his lips directly against her skin and his longing increased to such a pitch that he nearly shredded the hosiery getting it down her legs and off her feet.

Reining in his desire, he treated himself to a visual feast. She smoothed his brows with loving fingers as he took in every inch of her flesh, touching her at will, kissing, tasting. He leaned forward and nuzzled the delta of her womanhood.

"Grant," she gasped softly. He stood at once and lifted her in his arms, navigating the spiral staircase with ease.

He set her down next to the bed and flung back the covers. Smoldering lust and tender love combatted in his eyes as he laid her on the bed. With a brazenness she didn't know she possessed, for it had never manifested itself before, she propped herself up on one elbow to watch as he rid himself of his clothes.

As his brief underwear was peeled down his muscled thighs and calves she stared in fascination at his bold virility. He came to her slowly, not rushing, not wanting to frighten her.

Thus he was surprised when she said, "You're beautiful, Grant. Beautiful." Shy fingers reached out to touch his hard thigh. Then she leaned forward and kissed him, tentatively at first, then with an aggression that robbed him of breath, of thought, of life.

"My God, Shelley." Falling on the bed to lie beside her, he cradled her against him. The pressure of his hand on the small of her back urged her against him. The softness of her belly absorbed the strength of his desire and they pulsed together.

He stroked down her thigh with a leisure that brought a murmur of entreaty to her lips. He captured them with his own as his hand lovingly separated her thighs and touched the heart of her femininity.

His caress was tender and adoring. As it became more curious her arms tightened around his neck. Her breath was a soft wind in his ear as she sobbed joyfully, "I can't believe this is happening. Is it just another dream? Oh, God, don't let it be."

"It's real, my darling. You're real. Dear and precious and so very much a woman."

A gasp tore through her throat when he touched her in a way she'd never been touched before. Her heart and soul and mind expanded until they burst into a sparkling shower of light. "Grant—" she called, trying to pull him on top of her.

"No, my love," he whispered against her neck. "We share everything equally from the beginning."

His words meant nothing to her fogged brain then. All she knew was the glory of his hand sliding under the curve of her hips to bring her upward to receive his loving thrust. She took all of him, lifting her thigh over his and pressing him into her innermost self. She was washed with his fire. And what had happened but once in her life only seconds before, happened again, more sublime, more meaningful than the first time because he was inside her.

With their bodies still fused together, they lay in breathless repletion. Her hair was a damp silken skein that blanketed his chest. His hand idly caressed the contours of her back.

"Grant," she whispered, hesitant to interrupt this moment of bliss, "do you believe in fairy tales?"

He breathed deeply and she felt him awakening again, stirring within her body. "Not until tonight."

7

Grant studied the bite of scrambled egg on his fork and said contemplatively, "You haven't ever asked."

Shelley cocked her head to one side and looked at him quizzically. "About what?"

He chewed slowly for a moment, swallowed, took a sip of coffee, then said, "You've never once asked about Missy Lancaster and me."

She glanced down at her own empty plate. She didn't remember when food had tasted so good or when she'd been so hungry. After they had shared a shower, she'd wrapped herself in his royal blue velour robe. The garment, which hit him mid-thigh, came to the top of her knees. She'd prevailed on him to dress only in pajama bottoms.

Now, lifting her eyes to him across the first

breakfast they'd shared, she was again awed by how handsome he was. His hair was still damp from the shower. His cheeks were smooth from the recent shave. The hair on his torso curled and swirled in a pattern that continued to intrigue her though she'd traced it time and again during the night with slumbrous eyes and languid fingers. She recalled vividly the salty taste of the fine sheen of perspiration that covered him each time they made love. Her tongue had lifted it off his skin with dainty licks while he murmured love words and threaded his fingers through her hair.

The look she greeted him with now was warm and drowsy with remembrance. "It wasn't important to me to know. Nothing you did or could have done would have changed the way I feel about you. I thought that if you wanted me to know, you'd tell me without my having to ask."

He set his ironstone coffee cup in the matching saucer and reached across the table to cover her hands with his. "I have no idea what kind of lover Missy Lancaster was. I was never—never, Shelley—her lover. She was in love with someone else."

She digested this slowly. "Were you in love with *her?*" A ribbon of jealousy wound around her, squeezing her tight. She didn't want to know, but she had to know.

He smiled slightly and shook his head. "No. We were never more than friends. I've wished a thousand times I hadn't been such a good friend. Maybe if I hadn't been, she'd be alive." At her bewildered expression, he said, "Let me clarify. Missy was having an affair with a congressman. He was young, handsome, prominent, politically visible . . . and married, with three young children."

Shelley's frown revealed her opinion of the unnamed congressman.

"Exactly," Grant said, interpreting her expression correctly. "I thought her affections were misplaced, but she was crazy about this guy. Anyway" —he sighed—"when I joined Senator Lancaster's staff and met Missy, we developed a friendship. Grudgingly I consented to escort her to a reception where she was to meet her lover. After he'd commissioned someone to drive his wife home because 'something urgent had come up,' he sneaked Missy off to their rendezvous."

"And that first time set a pattern," Shelley said intuitively.

"Precisely. I found myself squiring one of Washington's prettiest young unattached women for the convenience of her lover. Either I'd pick her up at their rendezvous and take her home in the wee hours, or she'd get a cab. Either way, people drew the conclusion that it was I she was seeing and not the congressman with the lovely wife and three children."

Grant's disgust with the congressman was apparent. Obvious also was his disgust over his own culpability. "What happened?" she asked softly. "Why did Missy commit suicide?"

"The usual. She was pregnant and the congressman was furious when she told him. All along she'd foolishly expected him to leave his wife for her. I'd warned her for months that she was whistling in the dark, but she refused to listen. She called me from their secret apartment. When I got there she was disconsolate. He'd told her he'd arrange for a quiet abortion but that was all she could expect from him. When I dropped her at home, I advised her to go to bed and sleep on it. The next morning, she was dead."

She laid her hand on his. "Why didn't you tell anyone about this when you were unjustly accused and fired from your job? If you'd gone to the senator quietly and told him, wouldn't he have believed you?"

"Maybe. I don't know. If I hadn't named the guilty party, he might have thought I was making the whole thing up to protect myself. And if I had told him who the other man was, the senator might very well have confronted him. I would have enjoyed seeing the congressman get his comeuppance, but I didn't want to destroy his wife and kids. They were the only true innocents in the whole mess. Even Missy was old enough to know that you have to pay the piper."

"Few men would have done what you did, take the blame for something you didn't do."

He laughed harshly. "Don't pin any medals on me, Shelley. At that point my actions were guided by apathy, not integrity. I was fed up with the duplicity, the backbiting. If my colleagues believed I could be so callous, then I wanted no more to do with them. They were ready, even eager, to believe me guilty of destroying that girl's life. I just didn't give a damn anymore what they thought of me." He paused, and his vulnerability touched her heart.

"I went to Washington with stars in my eyes, with an almost fanatical respect for the government and the men who ran it. I found out in a short time that they're just men like the rest of us, with all the frailties of human nature. I came away feeling I was above all that." He fixed her with his gray-green eyes and said softly, "But I'm no better than any of them."

He pulled her to her feet and guided her around the small table until she stood in front of him. He clasped both her hands in his. "If you had come into my class a married woman, I doubt if it would have made any difference to me. Seeing you after ten years of separation, mature and more beautiful than ever, I wouldn't have let a husband stand in the way of my wanting you. I'd have done anything, said anything, to bring about what happened between us last night."

She touched the silver hair at his temples. Her voice vibrated with emotion. "You wouldn't have had to try very hard. Thank heaven I wasn't placed in the dilemma of having to choose between you and a husband. I'm not sure morality would have entered into my decision either."

"Your husband didn't appreciate the woman you are, Shelley. I know. I could tell by your surprised responses last night."

She smiled fondly at his male vanity. "If you mean he didn't love me well, you're right. He never loved my breasts with his mouth. He kissed them sometimes, but never as much as I wanted and never like you do." She never knew where this streak of uncharacteristic boldness came from, but she felt no self-consciousness about saying such things to him. "He didn't tickle the backs of my knees with his tongue, or talk to me when we were making love or snuggle afterward. He wasn't able to bring me to fulfillment, and he never forgave me for that. You did. All through the night."

He grabbed her hand and brought it to his mouth, kissing the palm fervently. "Thank you for telling me that, Shelley. God I wanted that to be the case. By your startled reaction, it seemed so. I *hoped* so. I'm a selfish bastard, but if I couldn't have your virginity, I wanted that."

She outlined the sculpted lines of his mouth with a loving finger. "The taking of my virginity meant nothing. It was painful for me, an act executed without love or tenderness. Last night was . . ." Her eyes searched the walls of the tiny kitchen as though she'd find the abstract idea she was searching for emblazoned on the walls. "Birth. I became a woman."

His eyes were filled with emotion. "I love you."

"I love you." She repeated his words softly. Then, because they had been withheld for ten years, she repeated them with more emphasis.

He drew her toward him and laid his head heavily on her breasts. Her arms enfolded his head and held it against her. For long moments they maintained that position, savoring their spoken avowals of love. When he raised his head his eyes issued an open invitation. "All this talk of knee kissing, etcetera, has made me . . . ah . . ." With deft hands, he untied the belt of his robe from around her narrow waist. The sides of the garment fell free, giving him an unrestricted view of her nakedness.

His hands stroked up the backs of her thighs beneath the robe while he lowered his head again and opened his mouth over her navel. His tongue delved into the soft indentation and he muttered, "Think you could get in the mood?" Were she not already quivering with desire, his mouth, hot and wet and urgent on her stomach, would have been strongly convincing. His hands cupped her derriere, lifting, tilting.

"I have a confession," she mumbled. "I thought of it before you did."

"Don't count on it."

"Let's go upstairs."

"Let's stay here."

He caught her off guard and before she knew what had happened, he had drawn her onto his lap. "Grant," she breathed, wide-eyed. "I've never . . ."

He winked mischievously, quite pleased with himself, as he yanked free the knot of the drawstring at his waist.

"You've always been . . . ah, Shelley . . . an excellent student, a fast . . . yes, that's it . . . learner," he strained to say through clenched teeth as she demonstrated an uncanny aptitude for innovation. She sheathed him with her dewy warmth and moved wantonly.

"You're . . . a good . . . instructor."

The dry, uninteresting contents of the finance textbook she was studying wouldn't register. For an hour she had tried to absorb the information she was reading, but her mind wasn't on it and her eyes seemed bent on wandering to the man sitting across the room, concentrating on the book resting in his lap.

She loved him so much, she was barely able to contain it. Grant's sexuality and her response to him stunned her. Daryl, well acquainted with the mechanics of human sexuality, had known nothing of romance, of a loving technique. He wouldn't have recognized the woman who had unabashedly participated in every act of loving with Grant as the same woman who had lain beneath him, apathetic and listless. It would crush him to know what a lousy lover he was. The thought gave her a perverse pleasure.

"You're staring." Grant's quietly spoken words brought her out of her daze and she made a face at him as he raised his eyes from his book.

"I'm studying."

"Um-huh," he said with obvious disbelief.

"I'd appreciate it if you wouldn't interrupt me again," she said primly. He grinned before going back to his own reading.

The weather, which was still cold and rainy, had encouraged them to stay indoors. They had returned to his bed after clearing the kitchen of their breakfast dishes. Sleeping for a while had refreshed them, but they'd agreed to be lazy for the remainder of the day. Each was jealous of this precious time they had been granted and didn't want anything to intrude on it.

She had reluctantly told him she had a finance

exam to study for. As he had to prepare his lectures for the coming week, they'd agreed to take two hours away from each other and study. As they stood in the middle of the room they played out a leave-taking scene that would have rivaled a tear-jerking movie.

"Let's sit together on the couch." He kissed her ear, his tongue detailing the outer rim.

"No. We'd never get our studying done and that would only prolong the misery."

"I promise not to touch."

"But I can't promise." She slipped her hands underneath his shirt and flattened her palms over his chest.

"But I'll be sitting way over there," he complained. "I'll miss you."

"It wouldn't work." She sighed, unbuttoning his shirt and kissing his chest.

"Are you afraid I'll distract you? Do something like this?" He dipped his head and flicked his tongue across her nipple. She was wearing an old shirt of his. He had convinced her she didn't want to dress in her stuffy suit again. With the shirt, which had the long sleeves rolled up to her elbows, she wore a pair of his white sport socks that came to just beneath her knees. The long shirttail reached to the middle of her thigh, providing only a modicum of protection.

When he pulled back, the soft cotton was wet where his mouth had been. "Or something distracting like this?" His fingers combed down her stomach, inched under the shirttail and found the dark V at the top of her thighs.

"Oh, Grant," she groaned and, with a supreme act of will, pushed him away. "Go!"

"Killjoy," he grumbled, but he went to the opposite end of the room and sank into a chair.

Now, over an hour later, she still knew no more about the exam material than she had earlier. Even at this distance, he continued to divert her. All she could concentrate on was his loving, the way his lips and hands could bring her to an apex of sensual excitement she'd never imagined. She should have guessed it would be this way between them. Hadn't the kiss of ten years ago, that forbidden kiss that had refused to be banished from her mind, hinted that no man would ever love her as he did?

She thought of the past affectionately. Of the future, she thought not at all. It frightened her. For where would they go from here? She wanted him. But devoting herself to a man was something she'd sworn never to do again. She loathed that person she had become when she was married to Daryl, for she'd lost her individuality. She had been a dim shadow, existing without nucleus, soul or spirit. Never again.

Grant had said that he loved her. But for how long? He hadn't spoken of a commitment. Was she only a tonic he was taking to restore himself after his debacle in Washington? Once healed, how would he feel about her?

"Now you're staring and frowning," he teased.

She blinked until he came into focus and her frown faded into a contented smile. If there was no future for them, she wasn't going to dwell on that fact in the present. She wasn't going to waste the time they had now ruminating about what might be.

"I'm sorry," she said, surrendering and slamming her book shut. "I was just thinking about the abysmal grade I'm going to make on that exam, and how it will be all your fault."

Having waited impatiently for the merest invitation from her, he vaulted out of his chair and came to stretch out beside her on the couch. "You might have to settle for a 'B.'" He claimed her mouth with a scorching kiss.

"Did you get your lectures outlined?" she managed to say when he at last released her mouth.

He ignored her and began kissing her neck. Her throat arched gracefully to allow him access. "I've been thinking. I may switch over to teaching anatomy and physiology. We'd have a helluva time doing research. You'd make straight 'A's.'"

"Would I?" she asked, her voice coming from deep in her throat. He had worked free the buttons on the shirt and was caressing her breasts tenderly. Cupping one, he lifted it slightly and closed his lips around the dusky crest.

"Um-huh," he hummed, not lifting his mouth, but tugging on her with exquisite sweetness.

Her hands slid down his back and curved over his jean-clad hips. At her encouragement, he settled himself between her thighs. With fumbling motions, she grappled with the fastener of his jeans. "Grant . . . ?"

"Yes, my love, yes . . ."

They froze when the doorbell pealed loudly.

He put his forehead against hers and let out a long sigh. The doorbell rang a second time. He looked down into her face apologetically. "Don't move," he commanded, levering himself off the couch and resnapping his jeans as he crossed to the door. He opened it no more than a few inches.

"Yes?" he barked.

A seductive giggle preceded Pru Zimmerman into the room. "Is that any way to greet a . . . friend?"

She turned toward the startled Grant before she could see Shelley, who was curled into the corner of the sofa, her feet tucked under her. She had hastily rebuttoned the shirt, though the fabric was twisted around her thighs in a telltale fashion.

Grant hadn't taken time to rebutton his shirt and Pru audaciously slid her fingers up and down the buttonholes as she said, "I came by to ask you about some extra reading. I didn't do as well on that test as I had hoped to."

Shelley couldn't believe the girl's gall. Her sweater was much too tight. Her breasts were unconfined, the nipples obvious through the knit. She moved closer to Grant with a swaying motion and tilted her head at an angle she no doubt thought irresistible. When her hand slipped into his open shirt, Shelley was seized by a fierce jealousy and cried out in anger.

At the same time, Grant's viselike fingers closed around the girl's wrist and jerked her hand away from him.

Pru whipped around toward Shelley and met her

turbulent blue eyes. She took in Shelley's dishabille at a glance. Fury thinned her petulant lips and narrowed her calculating eyes.

"Miss Zimmerman, I'm asking you politely not to come here or call again. Anything you have to see me about can be seen to in the classroom." Grant held himself rigid. Shelley suspected that if he'd let himself go, he would have throttled the young woman.

"Don't be ridiculous, *Mr. Chapman.* You know why I came here."

"Then I find your behavior not only rude, but offensive. I don't need to remind you that you're my student, nothing more."

"So is she," Pru screamed, pointing an accusing finger at Shelley, who was barely managing to control an impulse to fly at the girl and scratch her eyes out. She could gladly strangle her for touching Grant the way she had. "What's she doing here undressed and cozily curled up on your couch?"

"That's none of your damn business," Grant said heatedly. He gripped her shoulder hard and spun her toward the door. He opened the door with one hand while pushing her through it with the other.

"Well, I'll make it my business to see that Chancellor Martin finds out you're sleeping with your students," she threatened before Grant slammed the door in her face and clicked the lock decisively.

"Can you believe her?" Grant shouted, raking a frustrated hand through his already mussed hair. "I—Shelley?"

He had turned around to see her white, tense

face. Rather than quaking with rage as she had been doing but seconds ago, she was now cowering. "What is it?" he asked, rushing to her.

She swallowed. "Nothing, Grant. I think you should take me home." She began to get up, but his hands stayed her. He forced her face up to meet his eyes.

"Look at me," he demanded when she tried to avert her head. "Why? Why do you want me to take you home? *Why*, dammit?"

"Because . . . because . . . she's right, Grant. I shouldn't be here. People will think—"

"I don't give a damn what people will think," he roared.

"Well I do," she shouted back.

"Shelley . . ." His hands closed around her shoulders so tightly she winced. He eased his grip slightly. "I learned that no matter how circumspect you are, some people will jump at the chance to point a finger at you. People love to condemn others because it gives them a sense of self-righteousness. It gets you nowhere to try to please everybody. It's futile, impossible. You need only please yourself."

"No, Grant. I was taught early on that there are rules we have to live by whether we like them or not. We're breaking the rules. I've lived my life one way for twenty-seven years. I can't start changing now." It took every ounce of her self-discipline to look him in the eye and say, "If you won't drive me to campus to pick up my car, I'll walk."

He cursed viciously. "All right. Go upstairs and change."

They left the house within minutes. He ushered her out the door, locking it behind him. Impervious to the rain, he helped her into his car and backed out the driveway.

"My car's parked behind Haywood Hall," she said when he headed in the opposite direction from the campus.

"I'm hungry. I had planned on taking you to dinner tonight."

"Why? As payment for my favors?"

His head jerked around and she quailed under the sparks of anger shooting from his eyes. "Read it any way you like," he snarled.

She would have preferred that he slap her. At least then only her cheek would be smarting. Tears clouded her vision, matching the rain that pounded the windshield. She turned her head so he wouldn't see the effects their verbal dueling had had on her and proudly held her shoulders erect.

He drove to the outskirts of town to a popular steak house. Its rustic exterior blended into the backdrop of a rain-washed landscape. "I hope you like steak."

"Go to hell," she said, pushing open her door and dashing through the rain toward the door of the restaurant. If he thought etiquette had to be observed by buying her dinner, she wanted only to get it over with, so she could go home and nurse her wounds.

Inwardly, she shrank from the stormy expression on his face as he joined her under the covered porch and pulled open the door. His arm operated with the thrusting action of a piston. "Get inside," he said tensely. She shot him a seething look before marching past him.

A hostess led them to a table near the fireplace. "Can I get you something from the bar?" she asked.

"No. Yes." They answered in unison.

"Nothing for me," Shelley said with stiff dignity.

"Draft beer, please," Grant said.

The waitress left the menus and Shelley studied hers thoroughly until the woman returned with Grant's beer to take their order.

"Shelley?" he asked politely.

"I only want a salad. Vinaigrette dressing."

"She'll have a steak, too. A filet cooked medium. And a baked potato with all the trimmings. I'll have prime rib, medium rare, baked potato, too. Thousand Island dressing." He snapped the menu shut and handed it to the confused waitress, his eyes daring Shelley to contradict him.

She only shrugged and turned her head to stare into the fire. She remained resolutely silent during the entire meal, answering his direct questions politely but initiating no conversation. If this were nothing more than a payoff, she'd be damned before she'd let him enjoy it.

Once they were back in the car, he ground it into gear and spun out onto the rain-slicked highway. His increasing anger only served to feed hers. The earnest lover of the night before had vanished, and in his place was an angry, embittered man she didn't know.

A few blocks short of the campus he turned onto her street. "My car—"

"I know. It's at Haywood Hall. I don't want you driving in this weather, especially in a car—"

"I can take care of myself!" she yelled.

"I'm sure you can," he shouted back. "Indulge me, okay?"

He slammed on the brakes in front of her house and caught her arm before she opened the door. "Don't," was all he said, but the simple word was potent. With only a little indifference and a great deal of fear, she obeyed him and waited for him to come around and hold the door for her.

"Thank you for everything," she said with dripping sweetness before inserting the key in her front door and turning it.

"Not so fast," he said, catching the closing door with his boot and stepping inside behind her. "I'm not going to let you go into an empty house alone after you've been away overnight, no matter how well you can take care of yourself." He shut the door behind him and switched on the light.

He made a thorough inspection of her small house while she stood at the front door in growing irritation. When he strolled back into the room, obviously in no hurry to leave—indeed he had taken off his jacket and held it over his shoulder by his index finger—she said curtly, "Good night."

His grin was sly as he dropped his jacket onto a chair. "Good nights are usually said in the bedroom, Shelley." She stood in mute stupefaction as he came to her and yanked her against him, one arm going around her waist like a steel pincers. The other hand imbedded itself in her hair and pulled her head back as he leaned over her. "And they're usually accompanied by a kiss."

"No—" she barely got out before his mouth came down over hers. He kissed her without mercy, his tongue a marauder. Even though she struggled and squirmed against him, he lifted her easily and carried her kicking and thrashing into the bedroom.

She landed on the bed with an impact that drove the air from her lungs. He followed immediately, pinning her beneath him.

"Let me go." Tears of frustration mingled with those of despair as her fists pounded ineffectually on his chest.

"Not a chance." He locked her wrists into one of his fists. He fumbled with the buttons of her blouse and for the second time in twenty-four hours peeled down the silver slip to bare her breasts. "Tell me you don't like this. Don't want it. Don't need it." With his free hand, he caressed her. His touch was gentle, in direct contrast to the strength with which he held her.

"No, please don't," she moaned when she felt the rebellious response of her own body. Her head tossed back and forth on the pillow, but the fight was lost and she knew it. Her efforts were valiant, but without conviction. Her moans of protest became whimpering pleas as he stroked her now with his tongue. It flitted over her nipples in a caress like the rapid beating of a butterfly's wings.

At the first sign of her acquiescence, he released her hands. They burrowed into his hair, frantic now that he might be the one to escape.

"Shelley, Shelley," he breathed against her stomach as he pushed up her skirt and peeled the panty hose down her legs. He cursed them and his own clumsiness. Lest he terrify her with his desire, he forced himself to slow down, but her anxious hands on his shoulders were frantically imploring. He fastened his mouth on hers when his caressing fingers confirmed what he'd suspected. She was ready for him, pliant and moist.

He hurriedly freed himself from his restrictive clothing and poised on the threshold of her womanhood. He cradled her face between his hands and searched her eyes. "Do you think I'd let a stupid girl like that come between us? After ten heartbreaking years for both of us, do you think I'd let anything or anyone rob us of this happiness again?"

She shook her head, tears of love dampening her cheeks and the backs of his hands. "I told you that if I ever had you for one night, I'd never be able to let you go," he continued. "But I'll leave if you ask me to. I'll leave. Now. But you have to ask me to."

Her fingers intertwined behind his head and she pulled him down. She spoke against his lips. "No, Grant. Don't leave."

"Dinner. I didn't mean what I said about—"

"Neither did I. It was a stupid thing for me to say."

"I got rough. If I hurt you—"

"No, no," she moaned. "But love me now."

His body sank into hers, hard and full, filling the void his absence from her life had created and which only he could heal. Their tumult came quickly and simultaneously. As his life-force pumped into her, he said, "Nothing will separate us again."

And she believed him.

She awakened in a tangle of limbs. Grant's even breathing stirring the hair on the top of her head assured her that he was sleeping soundly. She eased away from him, covered his nakedness against the morning chill and crept to her closet to take out a fleecy robe.

Wrapping herself in it, she moved softly toward the kitchen with the intention of percolating coffee to carry in to him when he woke up. Musing on the tantalizing prospects of what would happen once they'd been fortified with caffeine, she was not immediately aware of the knocking on her front door. Puzzled as to who could be calling so early in the morning, she went to open it.

She peered through the tiny window at the side of the door and her heart lurched into her throat. "Daryl," she whispered in dismay.

8

He knocked again, more imperiously this time. For no other reason than to stop his insistent knocking, she unlocked the door and swung it open.

For long moments they stared across the threshold at each other. Shelley marveled over her supreme indifference at seeing him. Once, shortly after the divorce, the sight of him would have made her heart do somersaults. She would have been nervous, self-conscious. At one time he had possessed the power to make her feel insignificant. No longer.

As a sign of her newfound confidence, she made him speak first. "Shelley," he said, nodding his head with cold condescension. He was still handsome in a boyish, dimpled kind of way. "Did I get you up?"

"Yes," she lied. It gave her a sense of superiority to know that she was naked beneath the robe and that he couldn't arouse her body, never had been able to. She longed to shout that at him, to flaunt his failure, to debase and humiliate him as he had her the night he had emotionlessly informed her that he wanted her out of his life.

"May I come in?"

She shrugged and moved aside. He pushed past her brusquely and for the first time she noticed the anger that had kept his dimples from really showing. He was furious over something. He rarely let himself get so upset that it showed.

He turned toward her after only a sweeping glance around her living room. "Sit down," he said, flexing his fingers against his thighs, another sign of his agitation.

"No," she responded and crossed her arms over her chest. She couldn't imagine what had brought him from Oklahoma City so early on a Sunday morning, but she wasn't about to obey his commands as she once had. The only emotion he had aroused in her was curiosity. But she wouldn't even give him the satisfaction of asking what he wanted. She looked at him coolly.

His jaw tensed. He was grinding his teeth, a habit he'd tried for years to break. Once again his fingers were flexing as he held his arms stiffly at his sides. "I want to know what the hell you think you're doing?"

She blinked several times and laughed shortly. "I was about to make coffee."

He took a menacing step forward. "Don't play cute with me, dammit. You know what I'm talking about. That Chapman guy. Are you seeing him?"

She wondered distractedly how he could get the words past lips that didn't seem to move. "Yes," she answered simply. "I'm taking his poli-sci class twice a week."

"It's more than that," he roared, suddenly giving vent to his barely contained rage. "A friend of mine saw you at the football game and then later at the chancellor's house together. You've been going to his apartment in the evenings. What the hell do you think you're doing?" he demanded, repeating himself.

"That's none of your business," she said, flinging her head back in an attitude of defiance that he'd never seen before and that momentarily stunned him. The storm brewing in her blue eyes was new to him, too.

When he had regained his senses, he hissed, "The hell it's not. You're my—"

"*Ex*-wife, Dr. Robins. And at your choosing, if you'll remember. I don't know why you're here and care less, but I'm telling you now to leave."

He ignored her. "He's always been your dreamboat, hasn't he?" He sneered. "I don't think you realized how often you dropped his name. My God, seven, eight years after high school, who the hell remembers their teachers? But not you. 'Mr. Chapman this,' and 'Mr. Chapman that.' I only thought you were enthralled because he had gone to Washington. Now I know better, don't I? With his seedy reputation, I'd think your adolescent infatuation with him would be crushed. Or does what he did to that girl in Washington only make him more dashing?"

She wasn't going to defend Grant to this buffoon. Turning her back on him, she walked to the door and opened it. "Don't bother to come see me again, Daryl. Good-bye."

He strode across the room and slammed the door shut. Grabbing her shoulders, he shook her roughly. "Are you sleeping with him?"

"Yes," she emphasized, looking up at him triumphantly. "And loving every minute of it."

"You bitch," he lashed out, and Shelley knew she'd hurt him in the worst possible way. She'd punctured the ego that had needed deflating for years. He couldn't take it. "Do you know what a laughingstock you're making of yourself? Do you?" He shook her harder, but she never flinched.

"I'm making a laughingstock of you, Daryl, and that's what has got you upset. What did your friend do? Go back to the city and tell everyone that your pale, shy wife didn't look so pale and shy any longer? Did he tell everyone that she doesn't need you after all? That she's happier every hour of her life without you than you made her in five years? If so, he's right."

"Shut up," he shouted. "I don't give a damn what you do with your life, but I care how you affect mine. I've made a name for myself. I'm going to marry the chief of staff's daughter. Can you imagine what a match like that can mean to my career? But if word of your sleazy affair with your *professor* gets out, it could send all my career plans to hell in a handbasket. You'll stop this ridiculous affair immediately. At least until I'm married again."

She laughed up at him, making him all the madder. "*Your* name, *your* marriage, *your* career. Do you think I care about any of that?"

"You never did!"

"Oh yes, I did." She ground out the words. "I cared enough to work long, hard hours to support us while you finished medical school. I cared enough to do research for you and type your tedious, endless papers. But when you graduated third in your class, it wasn't me you thanked with a vacation or even a night out. You went on a three-day trip to Mexico with two of your classmates."

"I deserved a rest."

"So did I!"

"So the little stunt you're pulling now is to get back at me for all the injustices I heaped on you, is that it?"

She shook her head in incredulity. "Your ego never ceases to amaze me," she said laughing. "I wouldn't waste such precious energy on you. You can become the most famous doctor in the world, or you can rot in hell for all I care, Daryl Robins. You excised me from your life and it was the best thing that ever happened to me."

He leaned down closer to her. "It was the best

thing that ever happened to me, too. To think that I gave up my freedom to marry an iceberg like you. You played a gruesome joke on me, honey. Making me want you so much I married you, only to find out you're made of stone. I'll bet your professor was in for a shock, wasn't he? Or were you kind enough to warn him that making it with you is about as exciting as making it with a corpse?"

She paled, struck by his degrading words. But before she could form a comeback, he was yanked away from her and plastered to the wall. Grant's forearm was like an iron bar across Daryl's neck.

Bare-chested, having taken only enough time to pull on his jeans, he was barbarously fearsome. His hair fell over his forehead with primitive disregard for convention. Unshaven, his jaw looked even more determined. His eyes blazed into Daryl's face with pagan blood lust. "If you ever talk to her that way again, I'll wreak havoc on that pretty smile you put such great stock in," he growled.

Daryl swallowed nervously. Unsuccessfully, he tried bravado. "So you'd add assault and battery to all your other crimes."

Grant laughed, though there was no mirth in his smoldering eyes. "Say what you want about me. Insult me if it makes you feel better. Believe me, I've been bombarded by many bigger and better than you, Robins. You can't touch me. But I could easily kill you for talking to Shelley that way."

"What I said is true," Daryl squeaked out.

"What you said is trash. I wouldn't insult Shelley by giving you the details of our lovemaking, but I assure you it's the highest experience I've ever had in my life. And while you're lying in the cold sterile bed of your convenient marriage, I want you to think about all you're missing, all you threw away because of your monumental, misplaced self-esteem."

A warm glow burned inside Shelley, but it wasn't embarrassment over Grant's words; it was gratitude and love. She didn't even see Daryl's darting look in her direction. He looked at her with a new interest, but she only had eyes for Grant.

"Then you're going to continue your shoddy little affair?" Daryl asked on a deprecating note.

"No," Grant said softly.

Shelley's bubble of love burst and her eyes widened in alarm. Without lessening his hold on Daryl, Grant turned his head toward her. "No affair. We're going to be married."

Her lips parted in surprise but she didn't utter a sound. Daryl, too, was rendered speechless as Grant turned back to him.

"And I'm smarter than you are, Robins. I'll love her the way you were too stupid to. I respect her intelligence and ambition. Her career will be just as important as my own. The marriage will be a partnership. I'll make her forget the days she spent as your muddy doormat."

With one last threatening look, Grant released him. "Get out of here. You've spoiled our morning all you're going to."

Daryl almost slumped to the floor with relief. Recovering quickly, he straightened his coat and cast a disdainful glance at Shelley. "Congratulations," he said with cocky assurance. Then he made the mistake of turning his back on Grant.

"Oh, Robins?" Grant said pleasantly.

"Yeah?" the doctor said, belligerently facing him again.

"This is for all the times you brought her grief when I wasn't there to do something about it." Grant's fist shot out and buried itself in Daryl's stomach with a sickening thud.

The proud doctor bent at the waist, clutching his stomach. Mercilessly, Grant grabbed him by the collar, jerked him upright and dragged him to the door. He shoved him onto the porch and released him with as much respect for his dignity as one would give a dead rat.

Grant's epithets were imaginative and explicit as he closed the door and locked it. But as he turned back to Shelley his expression softened. His arms were outstretched as he approached her. A moment later she was enfolded within them and pulled against his furred chest.

His index finger tilted her head up and he looked down at her face lovingly. "It wasn't with candlelight and wine, I wasn't down on my knees, but it was a proposal just the same. Marry me, Shelley," he whispered urgently as he pressed her head into the curve of his shoulder.

Her arms went around him. She held him close, hugged him tightly. Squeezing her eyes shut in an effort to dispel Daryl's smirking face, to obliterate his debasing words from her memory, she said shakily, "I don't know, Grant. I just don't know."

He heard her indecision, understood her reluctance to get trapped again. Easing her away, he said gently, "Let's take a hike in the woods. This room still reeks of Robins. With any luck, once you're outdoors you'll see your way clear to marrying me."

"You're very quiet," he stated. At the caprice of the autumn wind, a golden-brown leaf had fallen on her cheek. He lifted it away with his little finger and stroked the curtain of hair that covered his lap.

"I'm thinking."

They had taken a country road out of town and driven in contemplative silence until Grant parked his car on the side of the narrow, tree-lined road. "Let's walk," he'd said. After taking an old blanket from behind the seat of the car, he had helped her over a shallow ditch and into a wood burnished to a golden luster by the cool fall weather.

The fallen leaves made a thick carpet that rustled with their footsteps. Even as they tacitly agreed to spread the blanket under a sprawling oak he respected her need for introspective thought. He hadn't pressed conversation on her.

She had lain with her head in his lap staring through the massive branches of the tree, not really thinking about what had transpired that morning, but enjoying the companionable silence, the strength of his thighs beneath her head, the whisper of his breath on her face.

"Good thoughts?" he asked, leaning over her now.

"Mostly."

"Want to tell me about them?"

"I was thinking that I feel better when I'm with you than I ever have in my life." She tilted her head back to see him better. "Do you know what I mean?"

"Yes."

"I want to be with you all the time."

"I fail to see the problem," he said when he heard the anguish in her voice. He threaded his fingers through her hair. "I've asked you to marry me, Shelley."

"I know, I know," she said, rising to a sitting position. She rested her forehead against her raised knees. "But I don't know if we should get married."

"I see," he said quietly. "Can you tell me why? Can we discuss it? Does it have anything to do with the scandal in Washington?"

"No, no." She shook her head dismally, though she didn't lift it. "I've told you that as far as I'm concerned, that never happened."

He placed his hand on her back beneath her sweat shirt, moved it up to the base of her neck, then all the way down to her waist. Back and forth, lovingly. "Are you worried about becoming a second-class citizen again?" Her hesitation in answering told him more than spoken words could have.

He removed his hand from under her top. "I've told you we'd be equal partners. Do you think I'd want you meek and submissive, Shelley? I want a wife and lover, not a live-in servant. You'd have the same status in the household as I. You've made your niche in the world and are going to make a bigger one. I'm proud of that. I want to enrich your life, not take your independence away."

Gently, he placed his hand beneath her chin and lifted her head. Her eyes were brimming with tears when they met his. "How is it that you're so understanding?" she asked huskily.

"I'm so much older and wiser than you," he said teasingly. When the corners of her mouth twitched with an answering smile, he said seriously, "Actually I'm not one of those men whose wife has to stay in the background so as not to threaten his ego. I can't see how your success, in whatever endeavor, could do anything but improve my life."

"What if I want to work my way up to be the president of a bank?"

"I'll be right behind you, giving you little boosts up the ladder if you should become discouraged." His hand slipped to her bottom and gently squeezed it. "A prospect I take delight in."

She blushed, more at what she was about to ask than at his display of affection. "And if I decide that I want to stay at home and . . . and maybe have a family?"

"I'll certainly do my part," he said solemnly, though his eyes were dancing, showing more green than gray. "What I'm trying to tell you, Shelley, is that I'll do anything to guarantee your happiness. I want you to be happy with me. I want us to be happy together."

To his surprise, her face crumpled and she turned

away from him again. "Shelley, for godsake what—"

"I want you to be happy with me, too, but I'm afraid I'll fail you," she sobbed softly.

"What are you talking about?" he asked with a combination of frustration and bewilderment.

"What Daryl said about me was true. Once we were married, I . . . I was like a corpse. I don't know what's happened to me these last few days, but I've never been this way before. Suppose we get married and I . . . disappoint you? I couldn't bear it. You've had so many women and—"

"Shelley, Shelley," he said, turning her around and cradling her against his chest. He ran his fingers under her hair, massaging the back of her neck with a loving hand. "Are you really going to listen to that strutting peacock and let anything he says get to you? My God, can't you see why he wanted to insult you like that?"

He raised her face to his and peered down into her confused, tear-filled eyes. "He knew that beneath your ladylike veneer was a passionate, sensual woman. I knew it ten years ago when I kissed you.

"What galled Robins and what will gall him for the rest of his miserable life is that he couldn't bring out that sensuality. The reason he came running here today wasn't so much that he thought our relationship could ruin his career; he was curious. Some masochistic compulsion drove him up here to see for himself if that sensual creature within you had finally been freed. One look at the woman you are now and he knew the truth. Being the coward he is, his only defense was to insult you, your femininity."

"But maybe he's right."

His smile was soft, knowing. "I'll prove to you how wrong he is." The rough quality in his voice gave it a special intimacy.

She stared at him, wide-eyed and trusting, as he leaned forward and kissed her fleetingly on the cheek. His lips nibbled along her cheekbone, her temple, pressed a sweet kiss onto her forehead.

He pulled back to survey the results of his work. "Your eyes are taking on that smoky hue that's a sure sign of your arousal. Even when you deny it, that cloudiness in your eyes is a dead giveaway."

All the while he was talking, he was rubbing her earlobes between his thumb and forefinger. Now he leaned toward her and kissed one, whisking his lips over it. Then he paused, stayed. His tongue batted at it playfully before he caught it between his straight white teeth and worried it tenderly.

She shivered and unconsciously placed her hands on his shoulders. He wouldn't be rushed. He gave the same avid attention to her other ear until she was twisting her head around in an attempt to capture his gifted mouth with her own.

When at last he obliged her, he sealed her mouth with his, joining them together and defying heaven and earth to try to break them apart. His tongue pressed deeply, explored thoroughly, evoking memories of the times they had loved.

"I love your mouth," he said urgently, dropping

hot kisses on her lips. "God, I love it. Every time I kiss you it's like eating a rich, creamy dessert." When he kissed her again, they reclined on the blanket. His hands slipped under her sweat shirt and he thrilled to the warm satin texture of her skin. With titillating slowness he stroked his way up her ribs to the undersides of her breasts. He cupped them, barely touching them.

Her breathing had become rapid and he smiled. He raised her sweat shirt and looked down at the sun-drenched radiance of her breasts. "How could you doubt your femininity when you have breasts like these?" he asked, softly chiding. "They're beautiful. Created for me to love." He traced a finger around one full mound. And again. And the circles became smaller until she was writhing against him.

"Kiss me," she rasped, clutching at air until she gained a handful of his hair.

He outlined her nipples with the tip of his tongue. Lifting his head, he studied their perfect response before he took one between his fingers to fondle and sucked the other into his mouth. As she was drawn deeper into the trance he was creating, her hips undulated on the blanket in a sexual ballet.

His hand caressed its way down to squeeze her upper thigh through the denim of her worn jeans. A cry escaped her lips. "Grant," she gasped.

His purpose wasn't to torment, but to please and he instantly reacted to her silent request. Raising himself above her, he stared into her befuddled eyes as he opened her jeans and slid his hand inside. The dainty lacy band of her panties was lifted and his fingers covered the dark downy triangle.

"Grant . . . ?" Her voice was thin and reedy as he parted and caressed.

"You are a woman, Shelley. I'll show you how much of a woman you are."

For only a heartbeat she resisted the persuasive talent of his fingers, until she saw that was a useless exercise. She surrendered to their sweet magic and the spell they wove. Delicately, tenderly, he stroked the very center of her femininity with a sensitive fingertip. A veritable mountain of fire built inside of her.

Restlessly she arched her back. Mindlessly she covered his dear hand with her own and pressed it. The mountain trembled with boiling internal pressure.

"Shelley, look at me," he urged as he gripped her other hand and interlaced their fingers. Her blank eyes opened to meet his and only then did they come into sharp focus.

"Grant . . . you are . . . ah, my love . . ." The mountain of fire erupted with volcanic intensity and she closed around his fingers spasmodically. The aftershocks went on and on until the conflagration burned itself out.

Her head lolled on the blanket even as her chest heaved with gasping breaths. When at last her pulse had slowed and her respiration had been partially restored, she opened her eyes again.

She blinked against the bright sunlight until he shaded her face with his lowering head. Drowsily she smiled at him. "I don't know whether to be thankful or ashamed," she said, barely above a whisper.

"Never be ashamed of what you are, and show your gratitude by never doubting that you please me. You're the only woman I want."

It came to her suddenly how selfish she'd been. She glanced quickly at the full evidence of his sex straining against his pants. Without weighing the consequences, she touched him. "I'm sorry. That wasn't quite fair to you."

He grinned and began unbuckling his belt. "We aren't done yet."

Feeling the exuberance of a naughty child, she laughed. "Grant, we can't," she said, even as he positioned himself above her. "Someone might accidentally see us."

"Nonsense." He ducked his head to blaze a trail of kisses along her neck. "Just relax."

"Relax? I can't," she said breathlessly, doing exactly that under the dictatorship of his mouth. "I've never made love outdoors before."

"No?"

"No, never."

"Neither have I," he admitted, "and it's high time we did."

9

Well?"

She loved the movement of his lips against her hair. "Well what?" She snuggled closer to him, relishing his warmth despite the impetuous love-making they had just concluded.

"Are you going to marry me?" He reached under the sweat shirt to fondle her breast. Only minutes ago she had lain uncovered and unprotected from his lips. His violence had been tempered by his love and she had welcomed his ravaging mouth. Now, she delighted in his tender stroking.

"I could be talked into it."

His thumb was gently soothing. "Please. I love you. This weekend has been incredible. I hope we have a thousand others like it. But an affair won't be enough for me, Shelley. I want us to share our lives, not just one facet of them. You're not the 'living together' type and I believe in commitment. Marry me, Shelley."

She moved her head so she could look up at him. "Are you sure, Grant? I'm a small-town girl, not cosmopolitan like the women you're used to."

He shook his head. "I wasn't nearly the man about town the press made me out to be after Missy's death. And even if I were, I want only you."

"I guess that settles it then," she said softly. His eyebrow wrinkled in query. "Because as long as I can remember, I've wanted only you."

Grant had little regard for the serene atmosphere of Chancellor Martin's office when he stormed through the door the next morning. Without even glancing around the carpeted outer office, he stalked to the receptionist's desk and, bracing his hands on it, leaned over her menacingly.

"I'm right on time," he said tightly.

The receptionist blinked at him through thick glasses and licked her thin lips. "He . . . he'll be with you as soon as he's seen Mrs. Robins."

With a nod of her silver-blue beehive hairdo, she indicated the only other person in the room. Shelley was seated against the wall in one of the uncomfortably austere chairs.

Grant spun around on his heel and spotted Shelley for the first time. His mouth thinned into a slash of anger. He tossed one deprecating glance at the receptionist, then crossed the cheerless room to

Shelley. Without the least embarrassment, he took her hand and held it tightly between his own as he sat down on the chair beside her.

"You got one too," he said quietly. He looked down at the monogrammed envelope that matched the one hand-delivered to him that morning. In it he had found a summons to appear in the chancellor's office at ten o'clock to review a matter of grave importance.

"Yes. A young man delivered it this morning. I tried to call you, but you'd already left your apartment."

"Are you all right?" He rubbed the back of her hand reassuringly with his thumb. His moss-colored eyes scanned her face anxiously.

"Yes," she said, smiling tenderly. "Though I didn't sleep too well."

When he had taken her home after their outing, they had agreed that he shouldn't stay at her house overnight; nor would it be wise for her to stay with him, until they were married. "Neither did I. I didn't have any place to put my hands."

"Shhhh," she said, blushing.

"I couldn't wait to see you this morning, then *this.*" He took the envelope from her hand and slapped it against his palm.

"What . . . uh . . ." She darted a hasty look at the receptionist, who wasn't making the slightest effort to disguise her interest. "What do you think this is about?" she asked in a hushed tone.

He looked at her with an expression of combined contrition and mischievousness. "You know damn well what it's about and so do I."

She nodded grimly. "Do you think Pru Zimmerman made good her threat?"

"Maybe. I'm sure she's going to try to hurt us one way or another." He thumped his thigh with a balled fist. "Dammit. I don't care what they think of me, it's just that I hate being treated like a fraternity pledge caught in a panty raid." She paled and he mumbled, "Sorry. Bad choice of words."

When they looked at each other and recalled the moments they had shared, they did something totally unexpected. They laughed. They laughed in pure delight with each other and their love. The receptionist's horrified expression made them laugh even harder.

She was still eyeing them warily when the intercom buzzer sounded. "Yes?" she said into the lighted panel. "Of course." Her watery eyes lit on Shelley. "Chancellor Martin wishes to see you first."

Shelley stood up, but Grant was right beside her. "He'll see us together," he contradicted, striding toward the forbidding door.

"Grant," Shelley said, grabbing his sleeve. "I don't mind. Really."

"I do. I won't have him browbeating you. We go together." He took another determined step, but she held him back.

"Belligerence may not be the best tack to take."

He turned to her and sighed ruefully. Then he smiled and maneuvered her toward the door with a less aggressive gait. "You're going to be good for me. In so many ways."

Chancellor Martin was seated behind his desk,

but he stood up as Shelley went through the door. He had arranged his features into a merciful countenance that hardened to disapproval when he saw Grant following her in.

"I asked to see Mrs. Robins alone."

"She's agreed that we should see you together, Chancellor Martin," Grant said. Stunned, Shelley turned around to see if she was with the same man who had been in the outer office. Grant's tone was respectful and humble.

Apparently the head of the university wasn't ready to forgive them, no matter how respectful Grant's tone. "Sit down, please," he said loftily.

Grant seated himself next to her after helping her into her chair. She crossed her legs and chastely tugged her skirt over her knees. Grant sat staring into the chancellor's stony face with polite interest.

"I had hoped that this discussion could be avoided," he began in his most judgmental voice—the king apologizing to the miscreant before lopping off his head. "Since this is a church-supported university, the world watches us closely, much more closely than it would academicians at a public university. Your . . . interest . . . in each other would probably be ignored anywhere else, but here, it has come under close scrutiny and criticism.

"You, Mr. Chapman, came to us with a cloud of suspicion already hanging over your head. Frankly, you've disappointed us. We—"

"In my teaching abilities?"

The chancellor seemed annoyed that Grant had broken his train of thought. "Uh . . . no. I'd be remiss if I didn't tell you that the chairman of your department finds your work commendable."

Grant smiled broadly and sighed with exaggerated relief. "That's good to know."

"However," Martin said sternly, "your moral code is as important at this university as your teaching ability." He peered at them severely, indicating that he'd come to the crux of the matter. "It was brought to the attention of one of our most generous . . . donors . . . that you have been cohabitating. We find that appalling and intolerable. He has threatened to withdraw a grant already designated for a new science building if you, Mrs. Robins, are not expelled and you, Mr. Grant, are not relieved of your post at the close of this semester."

"But—"

Grant caught Shelley's hand and stilled her angry outburst. "May I ask who our accuser is?"

"I don't see that his identity is important. He happens to be a very prominent physician in Oklahoma City. His daughter attended our university, as he did himself as an undergraduate."

Light dawned in Shelley's head. She looked at Grant to see if he shared her suspicions. His feral look revealed that he did. Somehow he managed to control himself. "I think I know of whom you speak and why such a busy, prominent doctor as you've described could possibly be interested in the love lives of two people he doesn't even know. You see, I've had the misfortune of meeting his future son-in-law."

The chancellor's fist crashed onto his desk. "Mr. Chapman—"

"Permit me," Grant said, holding up both palms. "Mrs. Robins and I are to be married next Sunday, Dr. Martin. I don't think we could demonstrate the way we feel about each other more clearly than that. Nowhere in my contract or in the bylaws of this university does it state that a teacher cannot marry the woman he loves. The fact that that woman is a student at this institution should have no bearing on the matter.

"You tell your 'generous donor' that if he wants to meddle further, I know some noted representatives of the press who would love to sink their teeth into such a story. Some of them feel that they owe me a favor. They went hard on me in Washington and a few of them have called me to say they've had second thoughts about the muckraking stories they wrote. They would love to relieve their consciences and make amends.

"It would only take one telephone call and the story of our upcoming wedding and the discriminatory attitude of this university would be smeared in headlines all over the country. You're afraid that our romance will damage the reputation of this university? I don't think you can begin to fathom the furor that that one telephone call could create.

"Think about it," he finished succinctly. Standing, he offered his hand to Shelley. "Shelley," he said, giving her one of his warm, reassuring smiles.

He drew her toward the door, but before they were halfway there, the chancellor stopped them. "Wait!" he exclaimed in a panicky voice.

Slowly they turned around to face him. He wet his lips with a nervous tongue and ran his palms down the sides of his coat as though to blot them. "I had no idea you were planning to be married. S-so soon. Of course, this sheds an entirely different light on the situation. Once it's explained to . . . uh . . . Dr. . . . the donor, I'm sure he'll understand."

He paused, hoping he'd be thanked. Grant stared back at him solemnly. Martin made an effort to smile, but it was unsuccessful. "Your chairman is most pleased with the way you're handling your classes, Mr. Chapman. We might even be persuaded to offer you an increase in salary once your contract is reviewed by the board." He wiped his hands on his coat again. "And as Mrs. Robins has been on the dean's list since her first semester, there was never any real possibility of her expulsion."

"Yes. That would have been ludicrous, wouldn't it? Good-bye, Chancellor."

"Chancellor Martin," Shelley said by way of good-bye as Grant held the door for her. When he closed it softly behind them, she turned to him and leaned against him weakly.

"Daryl. How could he?" she whispered.

"Because he's a selfish, petty bastard, that's why."

A scandalized gasp from the receptionist brought their attention to her. She was staring at them, her clawlike hand clutching at the material over her meager breast protectively.

"Oh, for godsake," Grant growled. "Let's get out of here before I do something rash."

The days went by quickly because they were both busy. Shelley attended her classes as usual and Grant had lectures to prepare and present. In his classroom, she maintained her seat near the back of the room, keeping a low profile.

They spent as many waking hours together as possible. Grant was only at his duplex long enough to pick up his mail and sleep away the remaining hours of the night after returning late from Shelley's house.

"I don't know why I'm paying rent," he told her. "The guy who lives next door told me someone was there looking for me today. Package delivery or something."

They had decided to sublet his apartment and live in her house until her graduation. "There's more space in your house," Grant said reasonably. "I can make that extra bedroom into an office."

"What about an office for me?"

"We'll share it."

"There's only room for one desk and chair."

"You can sit on my lap."

"No way."

"Okay, then I'll sit on your lap."

She was trying desperately to keep a straight face. "I may start thinking of you only as a sex object."

He grabbed her then, pulling her to him and

molding her to a body that was ever hungry for her. "Every guy should be so lucky."

Her parents were notified of the marriage and after the initial shock and a long, reassuring conversation with Grant, they promised to be in attendance Sunday afternoon.

Shelley was now completely confident in her decision to marry Grant. His loving thoughtfulness was nothing akin to Daryl's self-centeredness. Though Grant had a recklessness to his nature, a rebellious bent, she admitted that that was part of his attractiveness. She knew, too, that she wasn't harboring any adolescent infatuation. She was in love with the man, not with a fond memory of her youth. And they had even overcome the stigma attached to their relationship, if the silver tray sent by the board of directors as a wedding present were any indication.

Nothing could stand in the way of their happiness now.

"Oh, Grant!" she cried, stamping her foot.

He slumped against the doorframe, helpless with laughter.

"I thought you were my parents," she said crossly.

"Do I look that much older than you?"

"Don't be cute. You shouldn't be here. You're not supposed to see the bride before the wedding." She was barring his entrance into her house, wearing only a nightshirt that came to the middle of her thighs. Her hair was in curlers and she had a thick mint-green mask on her face.

"That's silly," he said, shoving past her. He was carrying a carton of books and a suitcase. "I had to start moving some of this stuff over. I'm going to live here, remember?"

"I don't know," she said, still agitated. "I may change my mind."

He only laughed. "I'll put these books in the spare bedroom."

"I'll wash my face, even if it is five minutes early," she grumbled, then called to him loudly: "Don't blame me if my complexion isn't radiant and blushing like a bride's. It'll be your fault."

"Your skin is glowing all over," he said awhile later. He had caught up with her in her bathroom after arranging his books in a bookcase they had set up for that purpose earlier in the week. She had rinsed her face and artfully applied her makeup. Now she was unwinding her hair from the curlers.

Catching sight of him in the mirror, she saw that he wasn't looking at her face, but at the bare skin of her thighs. The heated yearning in his eyes burned into her, fanning the coals of her own desire. "Maybe you should go in the other room and wait for my parents and your brother to arrive."

"I probably should," he agreed without conviction, watching each motion of the hairbrush as she dragged it through the thick strands of dark hair. He wasn't incognizant of the sway of her breasts under the nightshirt each time she moved her raised arms. "On the other hand, they're not due to arrive until noon. We have awhile."

She tore her eyes from his. It had been a week since they'd allowed themselves to make love, and if his hunger came anywhere near matching hers, it was gnawing at him like a ravenous monster. "You look nice," she said lamely, lightly misting control on her hair with a pump spray bottle.

His dark suit, light blue shirt and conservative tie looked incongruously formal in the intimate atmosphere of the bathroom. "Thank you," he said absently. He was studying her throat, counting each pulse that beat in the seductive hollow at its base. "So do you."

"I . . . I'm not dressed yet," she said breathlessly, turning around to face him.

"That's what I mean." His voice was rough with arousal. The pupils of his eyes were dilated so that they almost filled the irises. She saw herself mirrored in them, saw her arms lifting to encircle his neck.

"It's getting late. I ought to dress."

His arms went around her and he buried his face in the side of her neck. "Yes. By all means go dress. Don't let me keep you from doing something you ought to do."

All the while he was talking, his hands were lifting the hem of the nightshirt. First his fingers, then the palms of his hands glided under the waistband of her panties to cup her hips and draw her against his hardness.

Feverishly her mouth sought his and fused with it. As he pressed she rotated her hips over him, begging him to put an end to the craving that threatened to destroy her.

He lifted her and carried her to the bedroom, setting her down beside the bed. She wrestled with the buckle of his slender lizard belt until it came free, then unzipped his trousers. With trembling hands, she rid herself of the wispy swath of sheer nylon that had done little to deter his caress.

He loosened the knot of his tie and whipped it over his head after dropping his suit coat unceremoniously onto the floor. He stepped out of his pants, eased off his shoes and peeled off his socks, his eyes never leaving her as she lay back on the carpet and unbuttoned the nightshirt. He had only managed to undo half the buttons on his shirt when he collapsed to his knees.

Draping her thighs over his, he worshiped her first with his eyes, then with his touch, then with his lips. All the love he felt for her was made manifest in the sweet supplication of his mouth.

Endearments poured from two sets of lips in harmony, like a rehearsed chant. He knew the moment she could take no more and covered her with his hard chest, burying himself in her receptive body. Each thrust was a love song composed by his body for hers. His passion exploded at the moment she hurtled over the edge of the universe and their cries spiraled above them in a crescendo.

Replete, he slid down her length to rest his head on her breasts. Cradling it, she traced with adoring fingertips the planes of his face.

He raised himself enough to kiss her breast, gently sucking her nipple in a tribute to all that made her a woman. Then he looked up at her. The same lassitude he felt within himself was reflected in her slumbrous eyes, shining with love's completion.

His fingertip outlined the pouting fullness of her

lower lip and touched her dimples. "I don't know what to expect of the wedding," he whispered. "But the honeymoon is going to be terrific."

Shelley clipped on her pearl earrings as she hastened down the hall into the living room. Grant was already there greeting her parents. He shook hands with her father and spoke politely to her mother.

He had been retying his necktie when the doorbell chimed. He'd met her eyes in the mirror, which he was using over her shoulder. "One more kiss and we'd never have made it," he said teasingly. As he drew on his coat he kissed her fleetingly on the cheek. "You've got a smudge of mascara just beneath your left eye."

"And you've got a piece of carpet lint on your right lapel," she called to him in a stage whisper. He dusted it off as he raced across the bedroom.

She'd repaired the smudge, smoothed her hair, checked to see that she hadn't forgotten an essential garment in her haste, and then rushed to join them.

There was a flurry of activity and conversation as Shelley was embraced lovingly by both parents, complimented on her oyster silk suit with its teal blouse and presented with an armload of presents sent by hometown folks.

"Bill, that's my brother, is obviously running late," Grant said. "He and his wife are driving in from Tulsa."

Shelley was grateful for her parents' ready acceptance of her husband-to-be and the instant rapport among the three of them. "Would you like coffee?" she offered.

"Sounds good after that drive," her father said.

The doorbell and the telephone rang at the same time.

"I'll get the telephone and the coffee," Grant said. "You get the door. It's probably Bill, so introduce yourself." He hugged Shelley briefly, then rushed toward the kitchen.

When Shelley swung the door wide, her welcoming smile changed to an inquiring one. "Yes?" she asked the uniformed man standing on the covered porch.

"Is Mr. Grant Chapman here?"

"Yes. You are—"

"Sheriff's Deputy Carter, ma'am. May I see Mr. Chapman please?"

"That was Bill," Grant said, returning to the living room. "They're running late . . . What's this?"

"Mr. Chapman?" the deputy asked.

"Yes."

He placed a subpoena in Grant's hand. "What is this?" Grant repeated.

"A subpoena. You're to appear in civil court at ten o'clock Friday morning. There's been a suit filed against you."

"Court . . . suit?" Grant stammered. "What kind of suit?"

The deputy's eyes darted around the room. He took in the pretty young woman, the man looking every bit a bridegroom in his dark suit. There was a wedding present wrapped in paper sitting on the coffee table beside a florist's box with an orchid corsage inside its cellophane top.

He couldn't quite meet Grant's eyes when he said with a mixture of embarrassment and pity, "A paternity suit."

10

P-paternity suit!" Grant sputtered on a short laugh. "Is this a joke? Say, did the guys from the racketball club put you up to this?" He turned around to Shelley, smiling widely. "Those guys are—"

"I'm sorry, Mr. Chapman," Deputy Carter interrupted. "This is no joke."

Grant studied the deputy for a moment, then shook out the folds of the subpoena. His eyes scanned it rapidly, but its validity was quickly ascertained.

"Zimmerman," he ground out. "That conniving little bitch." His words were softly spoken, but they seemed to reverberate off the walls of the silent room.

"It's short notice, but we haven't been able to

reach you to serve the subpoena. I've been by your house several times. You're advised to contact an attorney—"

"I'll represent myself. Ten o'clock Friday?" The deputy nodded. "Forgive me if I don't say thanks."

"I'm sorry," the deputy said to Grant. Touching the brim of his hat, he nodded to Shelley and muttered, "Ma'am," before turning away and walking briskly down the sidewalk toward the official car parked at the curb.

Grant closed the door and released his breath in a long, weary sigh. "Helluva wedding present," he said bitterly as he turned. "God, Shelley, I'm—"

Seeing the stricken expression on her face was like being hit on the head with a sledgehammer. Her eyes were wide and vacant. The radiant complexion he had complimented her on only an hour earlier had blanched to a deathly white. A fine chalky line defined her lips, making the glossy coral lipstick look clownishly garish. She stood ramrod straight, but she was trembling, as though only her skin were holding her together, keeping her from flying into a million fragmented pieces.

"Shelley." His voice had a ragged edge. "Tell me you don't think . . . Tell me you don't believe I got that girl pregnant."

As though in a trance she shook her head, slowly at first, then more vigorously. "No," she said quickly, too quickly. "No." Her eyes blinked several times, then journeyed around the room aimlessly, focusing on nothing.

He took two long strides toward her and closed his hands around her shoulders. "Look at me," he demanded. She was held in his iron grip like a lifeless doll. "I didn't have anything to do with that girl." He pushed the words past clenched teeth. "Do you believe that?" He shook her slightly. Her arms flopped loosely at her sides, but her glazed eyes never wavered from his tight, furious face.

She wanted so badly to believe him. Of course he hadn't had anything to do with Pru Zimmerman, but . . . She'd been a young girl, too, the first time he'd kissed her. . . . And Missy Lancaster . . . Pregnant. He'd said Missy's baby wasn't his, that he hadn't been her lover. He wasn't lying. Couldn't be. He loved her. *Her,* Shelley. Still . . .

He took his hands off her shoulders, releasing her so quickly she nearly dropped to the floor. For a moment he stared at her averted face, disgust and heartache battling for supremacy. Shelley was never sure which was the victor.

He turned away from her and said to her father, "Bill was going to meet us at the chapel. I'll head him off there and cancel the ceremony."

When he turned back to her, she couldn't meet his eyes. At that moment she didn't feel anything. No anger, no pain, no disappointment, no despair. She was catatonic, completely void of feeling. Her spirit had deserted her, leaving behind a vast wasteland that once had been her heart.

When he left, Grant didn't slam the door. But the quiet click of its closing couldn't have sounded more final.

"Shelley, dear." Her mother was the first to break the funereal silence in the room. Shelley didn't know how long she'd been standing there, staring at the closed door. Her mother repeated her name.

Shelley lifted her head and saw that her parents were looking at her cautiously. Did they expect her to fly into a rage, gnash her teeth, tear at her hair, bang her head against the wall? Their wariness was justified. She felt capable of such acts. "I guess you drove down here for nothing." She laughed harshly. "It doesn't look like there's going to be a wedding."

Her parents stared back at her in sympathy. She couldn't stand their pitying expressions. It was like a reenactment of the days immediately following her divorce. "I think I'll lie down for . . . for a while." She began edging toward the hall, and by the time she left the room she was running.

She fell across the bed, hugging the pillow tight against her face as she screamed into it. Her body twisted against the excruciating pain of her soul. She vented her fury with tears and curses, pounding her fists into the mattress beneath her. Never had she succumbed to such a fit of temper, but then, never had her world been so unmercifully destroyed.

But the rage was soon spent, and she became exhausted. And the exhaustion was accompanied by despair, black and encompassing and absolute, suffocating her.

She rolled onto her back, heedless of the rumpled state of the carefully tailored silk suit. Her eyes stared sightlessly at the ceiling.

Why had she questioned Grant's innocence?

Suspicion had ruled her reactions. Why hadn't she been angry at the wiles of Pru Zimmerman and offered her support to Grant? That was what he had expected her to do.

But she hadn't. *Why?*

Because deep down she felt there was the slightest possibility that it might be true. She had told him repeatedly that the scandal with Missy Lancaster didn't matter to her, but apparently it did. The seeds of mistrust had been planted in her brain to burst into life with the first breath of uncertainty.

Could everyone else except her be wrong about him? That didn't seem likely. Was the love she'd always had for him blinding her to the duplicity of his true nature? Was she still no more than an infatuated teenager accepting everything he said as dogma?

She didn't think he'd been with Pru Zimmerman since she had become his assistant. The girl could be lying just to make good her threat to get even with him for spurning her. But Pru had felt comfortable enough at his duplex to waltz right in. . . .

"Oh, God," she cried and buried her face in the pillow again.

None of that made any sense. The way he'd looked at her from the first day he had spoken to her, the way they had loved so unrestrainedly that very afternoon, couldn't be misinterpreted. He must love her. Passion of that magnitude couldn't be faked.

For hours the thoughts swirled through her mind in a macabre dance. One moment she wanted to run to him, to beg his forgiveness for her lack of faith in him, the next she was remembering that he had kissed her when she was only sixteen. Missy Lancaster had been more than a decade younger than he. So was Pru.

In his mind, was she in the same category with them? *No, no.*

"Shelley?"

A light tapping on her door caused her to stir. Groggily she sat up on the edge of the bed. "Yes, Mom."

The door was opened and a wedge of light sliced across the room. When had it grown dark? "I thought you might like some tea."

She nodded absently. "Thank you. That sounds good."

Her mother set a tray on the bedside table. "Here, dear, let's get you out of that suit."

Within minutes she was lying between the sheets in a nightgown much more prim than the one she had planned to be sleeping in that night. She looked at the pillow beside hers, the one Grant would have used. A lone tear trickled down her cheek. Her mother took her hand and pressed it sympathetically.

"Go to sleep, dear. You need to sleep."

The dishes rattled slightly as her mother carried out the tea tray. When the room was plunged into darkness once more, Shelley soon found the oblivion of sleep too appealing to resist.

Her parents reluctantly left the next morning. They offered to stay with her for a few days, but Shelley preferred being alone. Feeling like a shell of a human body from which the heart and soul had been scraped, she maintained a solitary life for the next several days.

On the third day, she ate for the first time. She called friends in her various classes and asked for copies of their lecture notes, knowing that at some point in the future, she'd have to get on with the business of living again. She couldn't afford to get too far behind in her studies. The building of her career would be the only thing she had to look forward to.

When her classmates came by with the requested notes, she didn't invite them in, claiming she had a dreadful virus that her doctor said was highly contagious.

Her parents called every night and she strove to inject some animation into her voice so they wouldn't worry. Little did she know how forced her speech sounded.

It was with the same lethargy that Shelley pulled herself out of bed Friday morning. Mechanically she dragged herself into the kitchen and began to make unwanted coffee. When the phone rang, she reached to answer it without any interest.

"Shelley," her mother said peremptorily, "your father and I think you should come home for a few days. You've got to get out of that house."

She slumped against the counter. "No, mother. For the last time, I'll be all right. It'll just take awhile to get over him."

"I don't think so. You always had a special feeling for this man, didn't you, Shelley?" her mother asked softly.

"Yes, Mom. Always," she admitted.

Mrs. Browning sighed. "I thought so. That whole year, I think it was your junior year, he was all you talked about. When he left, you went into a decline, lost interest in everything. At first I didn't put two and two together, but when you continued to drop his name, always wistfully, I began to wonder. Eventually you seemed to recover and went away to college. I had forgotten all about him until he called that day. I was surprised to hear from him out of the blue like that. Once he'd introduced himself—"

Shelley pressed the telephone receiver closer to her ear. "He called?" she breathed. "He called? When? He came to Poshman Valley?"

Her mother recognized instantly the new alertness in Shelley's voice. "No, he telephoned from Oklahoma City. He said he had come down to the capital on an errand for one of the congressional representatives. I—"

"What did he want?"

"He . . . he asked about you, wanted to know what you were doing, where you were."

Shelley's heart had begun to pound. He hadn't forgotten about her! He'd called! She swallowed hard. "Mom, when was this? *What* was I doing? *Where* was I?"

"Oh gosh, Shelley, I don't remember. I think it was in the spring just after you married Daryl. Yes, I think so because I remember you and Daryl were talking about your quitting school to go to work and—"

"I was married. And you told Grant that?"

"Well, yes. I told him you were married and living in Norman. I'm surprised he never told you this."

Shelley's head dropped. She squeezed her eyes shut to block out the stabbing pain behind them. He had tried to contact her and she had already been married. He had been in Oklahoma City. So close. She'd only been married a few months. He'd gone back to Washington and she'd never known he had called. So close. If she hadn't been married she could have met him and . . . So close. If only . . . But it had been too late. Too late . . . *Then!*

Her eyes flashed open, her head snapped up, and the spiderwebs in her brain fell away. "What time is it?" she asked, glancing wildly at the wall clock. "Nine-forty. Good-bye, Mom, I'll call you later. I've got to hurry. Oh, and thanks!"

She threw down the telephone receiver and swept out of the room like a tornado, tearing off her robe as she ran across the living room.

"I'm going after him. Something I should have done a long time ago," she said to herself as she stepped into boots and pulled on a dress. Grant couldn't nave gotten that girl pregnant. "Besides that, he loves me. I know it."

She whirled into the bathroom to hastily apply her makeup. Luckily she had showered and washed her hair the night before.

"I've loved him for ten years," she said to the reflection in the mirror. "I should have gone to him directly after I graduated from high school and told him that. Gone straight to Washington to see him, or called him, or written him, but I didn't. A nice girl doesn't do things like that. She does what's expected of her. She marries an acceptable man whether she loves him or not. She goes with the flow and never swims upstream."

She had always loved Grant, but had lacked the courage to claim that love. All her life she'd been afraid of creating the tiniest ripple. This time, if she had to, she was going to make a wave.

"Young lady, you'd better have a very good reason for disrupting this meeting and barging your way in here," the judge said sternly.

"I do," Shelley stated without timidity. She looked directly at Pru Zimmerman. "She's lying. Mr. Chapman couldn't possibly have fathered her baby, if indeed she's pregnant."

After arriving at the courthouse, Shelley had discovered that the hearing was being held in the judge's chambers. Apparently the parties were going to try to settle the suit out of court.

Shelley had approached the court bailiff, handed him a note and insisted that she be allowed into the chambers as she had information pertinent to the lawsuit being reviewed. The bailiff was hesitant, but finally obliged her by taking the note inside.

She'd heard Grant's loud "No" of objection and the protests of Pru Zimmerman, but she'd been allowed to go in. Facing the querulous judge had caused her barely a qualm. Now that she had boldly made her statement, she felt a great sense of pride.

For the first time since she had entered the

judge's chambers, Shelley looked at Grant. His eyes telegraphed his love to her. She almost sank to the floor with relief that he didn't blame her for her temporary lack of trust.

"Miss Zimmerman is undeniably pregnant," the judge told her. "We have an affidavit to that effect from a reputable doctor, Mrs. Robins. On what do you base your statement?"

She straightened her shoulders. "Mr. Chapman has shown on several occasions that he has no interest in this girl. Miss Zimmerman came to his house once while I was there and pushed her way inside. Mr. Chapman insisted that she leave immediately and not come back. At that time she promised to get even with him for his rejection of her. I think this is her means to do so." She explained, too, about the time Pru had telephoned. "Mr. Chapman wasn't happy over the call. He didn't even want to talk to her."

"You're drawing conclusions, but I'll let that pass for now," he said. "On these occasions when you were at Mr. Chapman's house"—the judge cleared his throat—"were you there on a purely platonic basis?"

There was a heavy silence in the room. "No."

The judge's eyebrows shot upward. He then allowed a few ponderous moments to pass while he tapped a pencil against a stack of papers on his desk. He looked toward the table where Pru Zimmerman sat whispering with her attorney. Then his hawklike eyes slid to Grant.

"Mr. Chapman, I'm not unfamiliar with that unfortunate matter in Washington. Whether you were blameless in that affair or not has no bearing on this. However, once a man is implicated in a scandal, he is vulnerable to false accusations. I remind you that you are still under oath. Have you ever had carnal knowledge of Miss Zimmerman?"

"I have not." His voice was low, vibrant, firm, indisputable.

Pru Zimmerman squirmed in her chair when the judge pinned her with his stern eyes. "Well?"

Her face and her composure collapsed at the same time. She covered her face with her hands. "My boyfriend left me. I didn't know what to do. I'm sorry, I'm sorry."

The room was filled with confusion. While Pru's attorney led her from the chambers, she begged both Grant and Shelley to forgive her for lying. Finally, the judge recited the legal jargon that would officially dismiss the case against Grant.

When he was done, Grant lunged across the room, wrapped his hand around Shelley's arm and drew her to a more private spot near the window. His hands cupped her face and lifted it up to meet the love burning in his eyes. "Why did you put yourself through that? The truth would have come out in only a few short minutes."

"I wanted you to know how explicitly I trust you. How much I love you. Forgive me for letting you down when you needed my faith the most."

He kissed her gently on the mouth. "I'll admit I was mad as hell when I left your house, but I've had all week to think about it. One can't really blame a bride for getting upset when her groom is slapped with a paternity suit on the day of the wedding."

He laughed, but it was a sad sound. "God, I'm sorry, Shelley. If we live to be a hundred years old, I'll never be able to make that up to you."

"You already have. By loving me."

"But this may not be the last time something like this happens. As the judge said, my character and reputation will be suspect for a long time."

"I can handle anything as long as I know you love me."

"I do." He clasped her to him as though he wanted to make her part of his body.

"Grant, why didn't you tell me you had called asking for me years ago?"

He straightened to look down at her. "How did you know about that?"

"Mother accidentally told me this morning. Why didn't you tell me that at the beginning?"

"I was afraid you might think I was grandstanding. Or you might have thought I was clinging to the past and not seeing you as the woman you are now. Once I knew how you felt about me, I hesitated to tell you. You were bitter enough about your marriage. I didn't want you lamenting over things that might have been."

"I'll always regret the years we wasted apart, regret that I didn't let you know what I felt once I was old enough to realize it wasn't merely idol worship."

"Let's not waste any more time," he whispered, raking his lips across hers.

"What do you mean?"

"Judge?" he called to the man who was straightening his desk. The judge looked up, surprised to see them now that everyone else had left. "Would you do us a favor? Would you marry us?"

"You don't look like any banker I've ever seen," Grant drawled from the door of the bathroom as she stepped out of the shower.

"And you just love telling me that," she said, flicking her fingers close to his face and sprinkling it with water.

He took the towel out of her hand and tossed it on the floor. "Let's just say I've never had a lech for a loan officer before. I've never had the urge to do this." He covered her breast with his hand and rotated the palm over the puckering nipple. "Nor have I ever seen a banker carrying a sweet little bundle like this." His other hand smoothed over the gentle swelling of her abdomen.

"It's not so little anymore," she said against the warm masculine skin of his throat.

"Do they make maternity clothes in conservative gray pinstripes?"

"I hate conservative gray pinstripes as much as you do. No one has complained about my maternity clothes. It gives my women customers confidence to see a woman combining a career and motherhood."

Four months of pregnancy had made little difference in her body except for the obviously healthy growth of the infant and the fullness of her breasts, both of which delighted the expectant father. Grant's hands explored her abdomen each day, measuring the progress of their child.

"I love him already," he said, kissing the still

supple skin of her abdomen. "But not quite as much as I love his mother," he whispered, straightening up far enough to kiss the deep cleft between her breasts.

"Even after three years of marriage?"

"Has it been that long?" His mind wasn't on the conversation. He was lazily testing the texture of her nipple against his tongue.

She purred and slipped her hand past the waistband of his trousers. "Yes, and I'm still fighting coeds off you."

"Naw," he scoffed with what breath was left him.

"Oh yes. They can be hot-blooded, too. I know what it's like to sit in a classroom and lust after the teacher."

"You do?"

"Um-huh."

After her graduation, they had moved from Cedarwood to Tulsa where she had secured a prestigious position in a bank. Grant had begun teaching at a noted state college and within two years had become chairman of the political-science and prelaw department. He was still as ruggedly handsome as ever, trim and athletic. The additional silver in his hair only heightened his attractiveness.

For their first Christmas together, she'd given him a pipe and a tweed jacket with suede patches on the elbows. He'd looked up from the unwrapped present with ill-disguised disappointment. "No professor should be without them," she'd said teasingly. On December 26 he'd exchanged them for a leather battle jacket and a tight pair of jeans. Grudgingly, she had admitted that they were an improvement over her selections, but she glared at every woman on campus who dared to appreciate his sex appeal overtly.

Now and then fragmented accounts of the Lancaster scandal would surface, but the details of it grew dim in public memory. Grant was admired for what he was now. The shadowy past had little influence on the respect he presently commanded. Indeed, he'd been asked to consider running for the state legislature.

"Do you want to?" Shelley had asked in delight when he'd informed her of the political-party committee that had approached him.

"I wouldn't be opposed to becoming involved on a local or even a state level. Maybe if we inject some integrity into state politics, some of the muck I saw in Washington will clear up."

He was still considering it and she had made it clear that whatever his decision, she was behind him all the way. Her life was full to overflowing. The years with Daryl, who they had read was already divorced from his second wife, might never have been. Her life had begun the day Grant Chapman had invited her for coffee after his political-science class. Or rather, the day he had kissed her the first time when she was still in high school. Those dismal years in between had almost been erased from her memory.

Now, as he held her, all the love she had for him went into her ardent caress. "Shelley," he gasped. "Since you're not behaving at all like a reserved banker should, I'm going to have to unzip my pants."

"Why don't you just take them off," she suggested with a sultry voice and a lascivious wink. Their hands competed over whose could move the fastest, until he was as naked as she.

"Got any more good ideas?" he asked in her ear as he slid his hand between her slender thighs.

"Um-huh," she hummed. She touched him again, rubbing him against her own body.

He sighed her name as he lifted her and carried her into the bedroom. Laying her gently on the bed, he came down beside her, facing her. She nuzzled her face against the crinkly dark hair on his chest. Her mouth moved seductively. Daintily she caressed him with her tongue.

"Shelley, you're . . . yes . . . sweet. . . ."

She lifted her head for the glory of his deep, plundering kiss. As ever, it robbed her of breath, of reason. The cords of her body began to vibrate like the strings of a finely tuned harp. She closed her lips around his tongue as it roamed her mouth, tasting her, gathering her essence and making it his.

His hands cupped her breasts, lifting them and pressing them together. He lowered his head and praised the new dusky color of the sensitive nipples.

"Grant, love me," she beseeched him as he joined their two bodies into one.

Embedded deep inside her, he rocked them toward the sublime. "This is the way I first made love to you," he said. "Remember, Shelley?"

"Yes, yes," she said against his mouth as she felt herself slipping into the velvet oblivion. "I remember."

Silhouette Desire

Coming Next Month

So Sweet A Madness by Suzanne Simms

Taylor Jameson was an arresting sight and Detective Adam McCord vowed to make her his. Only Taylor was convinced there was no room in her life for a man, until Adam's strong arms reached out to claim her love.

Fire And Ice by Diana Palmer

Cal Van Dyne vowed that Margie's sister wouldn't marry his brother, but Margie was just as determined that the wedding would take place. Too late she discovered that, not only was Cal a formidable adversary, but a passionate one as well!

Opening Bid by Marilyn Kennedy

As a successful art dealer, Joanna Dillon prided herself on taking home the best pieces from every auction—until Phillipe Morceau stepped into her life. He outbid her at the auction; but would he also win her heart?